It's like a really bad *dream come true.* . . .

Johnny's arms flailed and he let out a strangled cry of alarm.

"Think he was telling the truth?" Mandy asked. "I mean, that he wasn't a good swimmer?"

"I don't know," Jessica said, watching him thrash around. "But it shouldn't matter. The water's only four feet deep there."

"Help!" Johnny yelled, slapping at the water with his hands.

"I think you'd better go in there and help him," Mandy said.

Johnny flopped and gasped like a fish. "Help!" he gargled.

Jessica managed to grab him around the chest. It was like wrestling a dolphin. "Put your feet down!" she told him.

"Help!" Johnny screamed again.

"I *am* helping," Jessica said in a reasonable tone. "Just put your feet down."

"I'll sink," he protested.

"No you won't," Jessica argued. "*I'm* standing up and you're lots taller than I am."

Bantam Books in THE UNICORN CLUB series.
Ask your bookseller for the books you have missed.

Visit the Official Sweet Valley Web Site on the Internet at:

http://www.sweetvalley.com

THE UNICORN CLUB®

JESSICA'S DREAM DATE

Written by
Alice Nicole Johansson

Created by
FRANCINE PASCAL

BANTAM BOOKS
NEW YORK • TORONTO • LONDON • SYDNEY • AUCKLAND

RL 4, 008-012

JESSICA'S DREAM DATE
A Bantam Book / February 1998

Sweet Valley High® and The Unicorn Club®
are registered trademarks of Francine Pascal.

Conceived by Francine Pascal.

Produced by Daniel Weiss Associates, Inc.
33 West 17th Street
New York, NY 10011.

Cover art by Bruce Emmett.

ISBN: 0-553-48608-X
Published simultaneously in the United States and Canada

Bantam Books are published by Bantam Books, a division of Bantam
Doubleday Dell Publishing Group, Inc. Its trademark, consisting of the
words "Bantam Books" and the portrayal of a rooster, is Registered in U.S.
Patent and Trademark Office and in other countries. Marca Registrada.
Bantam Books, 1540 Broadway, New York, New York 10036.

PRINTED IN THE UNITED STATES OF AMERICA

OPM   0 9 8 7 6 5 4 3 2 1

To Christopher Metsos

One

"Jessica!" Kimberly Haver hissed. "Don't do that. We'll get into trouble."

Jessica Wakefield ignored Kimberly's warning. She continued scraping at the corner of the large Johnny Buck poster pasted on the brick wall outside the Sweet Valley Bakery.

"Jessica!" Kimberly hissed again. "Stop!"

Jessica tossed her long blond hair off her shoulders and glanced both ways with large blue-green eyes. The sidewalk was empty. "Just keep your eye out and tell me if you see somebody coming," she told Kimberly, working carefully to avoid tearing the poster.

Kimberly let out a little nervous breath of impatience. "I can't *believe* you're doing this."

"Shhh," Jessica said. She was nervous enough.

She didn't need Kimberly making her even more anxious. If she didn't keep her hands steady, she might rip part of Johnny's face. Jessica tugged gently, breaking the glue seal around the borders.

Kimberly shifted her weight from one hip to the other and kept a fidgeting watch. "Stealing posters is probably a crime or something," she said.

"I've seen about a thousand million of these posters around town. They won't miss one and it'll look fantastic on the wall of my bedroom." Once the glue seal was broken all around, the poster peeled easily away from the wall. Jessica removed it intact with a little screech of triumph. "Yes!" She rolled up the poster and tucked it under her arm. "Let's go," she said, tugging on Kimberly's sleeve just as two women came out of the bakery with large packages.

Giggling, the girls ran around the corner to Casey's Soda Shop. The Unicorn Club was meeting there to watch *Sweet Talk*, the hip teen talk and video show. Today's show was a special one. The winner of the "Meet Johnny Buck" contest was going to be announced.

Jessica peered through the window of Casey's. Ellen Riteman, Lila Fowler, Rachel Grant, and Mandy Miller sat at their favorite table near the counter, spooning up big bites of mint vanilla and chocolate chip cookie dough sundaes—a Casey's specialty.

Kimberly pulled the door open and Jessica

followed her inside, eager to show off her trophy.

"Wow!" Kimberly commented. "Good crowd today."

Jessica looked around. Every table was full. On the other side of the soda shop, she saw her identical twin sister, Elizabeth, sitting with her friends, Maria Slater, Evie Kim, and Mary Wallace. They were a club too. They called themselves the Angels.

"Look." Jessica nudged her arm. "A lot of the guys are here. There's Rick and Aaron."

"I guess even they're psyched to find out who won the contest," Kimberly responded.

"That's 'cause Johnny's the kind of star that guys *and* girls like. He rides a motorcycle and he's athletic. Besides, this is an *event* for Sweet Valley. Everybody wants to be part of it," Jessica gushed.

Johnny Buck was coming to Sweet Valley to put on a benefit concert for the Sweet Valley Children's Hospital. The hospital was one of the country's leading research facilities for pediatric cancer. It specialized in treating difficult cases. The hospital also provided medical care for lots of kids who were poor and had no place else to go for help.

Sweet Talk had been promoting the benefit for the last two months. The concert had already raised thousands of dollars in advance ticket sales.

As a special promotion, *Sweet Talk* had also encouraged all the Johnny Buck fans in Sweet Valley to send in a postcard with their name, address, and phone number. The winner would get to meet

Johnny Buck and show him around town when he arrived.

Of course, all the Unicorns had sent in their entries—along with every other middle schooler in Sweet Valley.

Jessica and Kimberly hurried to join the other Unicorns. "Ta da!" Jessica sang before unfurling the poster like a banner.

Ellen Riteman shrieked and clutched Mandy Miller's arm. "It's him. I think I'm going to faint."

Mandy giggled. "I'm not the fainting type, but if I were, I'd definitely faint over Johnny Buck."

"Cool!" Rachel Grant exclaimed. "Where did you get it?"

"I refuse to answer that question on the grounds that it might incriminate me," Jessica answered dramatically. She plopped into a chair and rolled her prize back up.

"I want one," Lila Fowler said. "I'll buy it from you."

Jessica shook her head. "Nope. Not for sale. I'm going to get Johnny Buck to autograph it."

"Like you'll really be able to get close enough," Rachel scoffed.

Jessica smiled. "I'll figure out a way."

"That's what I'm afraid of," Lila groaned. "Please, Jessica. Don't embarrass me."

"You're just jealous of my poster," Jessica accused.

"*Me?*" Lila squeaked. "It's *you* who's jealous of

me. Because I'm the one who has the pull."

Lila Fowler's dad was one of the richest men in California and was on the board of the hospital. He had been given VIP passes to the benefit, and Lila had invited all the Unicorns to sit with her in the front section of the Sweet Valley Auditorium. She hadn't stopped talking about her own generosity for two weeks.

Rachel finished her sundae with a gulp and looked at her watch. "It's getting close to zero hour," she told the others. "*Sweet Talk* should be starting any minute now."

"Let's have a group wish," Mandy suggested.

"For what?" Ellen asked.

"That one of us will win," Mandy answered, rolling her eyes as if she couldn't believe Ellen even had to ask. She lifted her water glass. "Here's to the Unicorns. May the best fan win and *please* let it be one of us." The group executed a six-way toast.

Please let it be me, Jessica thought as she clinked her glass against Rachel's.

Jessica had a super-gargantuan-bigger-than-the-whole-galaxy crush on Johnny Buck. Lots of girls had crushes on Johnny, but Jessica knew her crush was bigger and more gargantuan than anybody else's. Whenever she looked at his picture, her heart beat faster. Hearing his voice on the radio made her feel weak in the knees.

He was the handsomest, coolest, most talented guy in the whole world—and the nicest. Only a real humanitarian would take the time to do a free concert for the hospital.

Jessica hugged the poster a little closer to her heart and tried to send a little extrastrength wish into the universe.

Maria Slater stood on a chair so she could reach the TV that was mounted on the wall. "Anybody mind if I turn on *Sweet Talk*?" she asked in a teasing voice.

Everybody in Casey's applauded and whistled their approval.

"Turn it up loud so we can all hear the Buckster," Rick Hunter called out.

Maria turned the dial to the right channel and cranked up the volume until it boomed through Casey's.

An advertisement for acne medicine was on and some of the boys began to make fun of the commercial. When the TV screen showed a close-up of a blemish, Rick Hunter let out a bloodcurdling scream.

Several people laughed, including Mandy and Rachel. Other people shushed him, and shouts of "Be quiet" rang out as the commercial ended and the theme song of *Sweet Talk* pounded through the room.

The theme song was a few bars of Johnny Buck's Grammy-winning hit song, "Meet Me in the Front Yard." Bobby Carroway, the really cute teen host of the show, ran onstage and smiled and bowed until the applause from the studio audience died down.

Jessica pulled her leg up and sat on her ankle so that she could see better over Lila's head. Usually she liked listening to Bobby Carroway. He was funny. But today, it seemed as if his opening remarks went on and on forever. She wasn't the only one who felt that way.

"Hurry up," she heard Kimberly urge under her breath. "We want to see Johnny Buck."

Jessica glanced around the soda shop. Every face was shining with eager anticipation. Some lucky Sweet Valley teen was going to get to meet the Buckster and actually spend the day with him.

"Before we bring Johnny Buck out," Bobby was saying, "let's take a look at his latest video for his new hit song—'Messenger of Love'."

"Boo!" Rick Hunter shouted. "We want to see Johnny rock."

The rest of the kids in the soda shop shushed him. Johnny Buck could rock with the best of them, but his romantic ballads were what had made him famous.

The video came on and every girl in the shop including Jessica sighed out loud as the sound of his deep voice filled the room.

The video showed Johnny riding into a town on a big black motorcycle. He drove past a beautiful girl with long blond hair. She watched his motorcycle drive by and the camera closed in on her face. Then the picture faded to another scene.

Johnny Buck stood on top of a tall cliff wearing a pair of jeans and no shirt. His wavy hair was tousled by the breeze. He lifted his arms and dove gracefully into a waterfall that poured into a foaming river.

The song went on and Johnny surfaced beside the beautiful girl. They exchanged a smile, then swam together toward the shore.

The next scene showed Johnny riding a horse bareback. The girl sat behind him with her arms wrapped around his waist. It was so romantic and cool, Jessica actually shivered and broke out in goose bumps.

"Wow! Can you imagine what it would be like to be that girl?" Mandy whispered.

"Yes," Jessica answered. She *could* imagine because she'd had a lot of practice. Jessica spent hours at a time daydreaming about herself with Johnny Buck.

Jessica pictured herself swimming with Johnny Buck and riding behind him on a beautiful horse. Then she imagined walking hand in hand with him down a quaint street—just like the couple was doing in the video.

The video was ending. Johnny put his fingers under the girl's chin and kissed her softly. The camera pulled back and Johnny climbed onto the big motorcycle and roared away. The girl watched him disappear down the road and waved.

The credits began to roll. The name of the song scrolled across the screen and moments later the video was over.

"How totally and completely romantic," Ellen gasped, chewing on a cuticle. "If only stuff like that could happen in real life."

Bobby Carroway smiled into the camera. "That was 'Messenger of Love.' A great song. And a great video. And now it's time to meet a great man. Let's have a big hand for . . . *Johnnyyyyy Buck!*"

The soda shop erupted into applause as the kids clapped along with the TV studio audience. Johnny Buck ran onto the *Sweet Talk* stage and shook Bobby's hand.

"I love those jeans," Kimberly groaned. "Are they the coolest or what?"

Johnny wore dark blue boot-cut jeans with black boots and a black shirt. A wisp of hair was pulled down over his forehead and a silver earring dangled from one ear.

"So Johnny," Bobby said. "Welcome to *Sweet Talk*."

"Thank you for having me," Johnny said graciously. "I really appreciate the chance to come on and talk about something that means a lot to me, and that's the Sweet Valley Children's Hospital."

Johnny smiled into the camera. "The Sweet Valley Children's Hospital is one of the best in the country and deserves everybody's support. I'll be in Sweet Valley next Saturday to rock 'n' roll. And I want everybody there to turn out and support the cause." He lifted his fist—his trademark Johnny Buck gesture.

Everybody in the soda shop lifted their fists and cheered to show their support.

"Have you ever been to Sweet Valley?" Bobby asked Johnny.

Johnny nodded. "Sure. I've done concerts there before, but I've never had the chance to really see the town. And this time, not only am I going to get a tour, but I'm going to meet one of my Sweet Valley fans."

There was a drumroll and Bobby ran offstage. He returned pushing a huge glass cylinder mounted on wheels. The cylinder was filled with postcards.

Jessica's stomach knotted in anticipation.

Bobby invited Johnny to turn the handle on the end of the cylinder. Johnny turned it round and round. All the postcards fluttered and tumbled around inside. The drumroll grew more intense. Jessica felt butterflies flutter and tumble inside her stomach just like the postcards in the cylinder.

One of those cards had her name on it. *Pick mine*, she mentally begged. *Please!*

The large cylinder came to a stop. Johnny opened a small hatch and reached inside. The soda shop was so quiet, you could hear a pin drop. Every single person was holding his or her breath.

Johnny Buck plucked a postcard from the hundreds of entries and held it up. The drumroll ended with a cymbal crash. The camera zoomed in on Johnny Buck while he read the postcard. Then he tucked his chin and smiled into the lens, his deep blue eyes twinkling. "I'll be seeing you soon . . . *Jessica Wakefield!*"

There was a moment of stunned silence. Jessica

shook her head. Had she heard him correctly?

Then she felt Kimberly's fingers clutch at her sleeve and pull her to her feet. "You won! You won!" Kimberly screamed.

Mandy, Ellen, and Rachel leaped out of their chairs and into one another's arms, jumping up and down and squealing with happiness. The other kids in the soda shop began to hoot and stamp their feet.

Even the Angels were jumping up and down with excitement. Elizabeth ran over and hugged Jessica tightly.

"This is *unbelievable!*" Ellen Riteman yelled, shimmying to the music.

"Unbelievably unbelievable!" Rachel Grant confirmed, jumping on her chair and lifting her arms like an Olympic track winner completing a victory lap.

Jessica stared at the screen. Johnny Buck was still talking—talking right to her it seemed. Through the haze of cheers, laughter, and excited chatter, Jessica heard him say, "Jessica Wakefield, I'll be in touch." He pointed toward the camera and winked.

Jessica's knees wobbled and she sank into her chair. *Right now, I'm the happiest thirteen-year-old in the entire world,* she thought blissfully.

She looked at Lila's face. Lila was smiling, but Jessica could tell it was a forced smile.

Lila was Jessica's best friend and fiercest rival.

No matter what Jessica did, Lila usually managed to eclipse her. It bugged Jessica a lot, but usually there was nothing she could do about it—until now.

Lila had been preening and bragging about getting the group VIP passes to the concert. But this was going to blow Lila Fowler and her VIP passes right out of the water. No matter what Lila did for the rest of her life, nothing could compare with having a day—a *date*, if you wanted to get technical—with the most handsome, most athletic, most talented, and most warmhearted guy in the whole wide world.

Two

"You're out of your mind," Steven Wakefield said the next morning in a scornful tone. "Johnny Buck is like, way older than you. He's not going to be interested in a little kid."

Jessica scowled at her fifteen-year-old brother across the breakfast table. "I'm not a little kid! Besides, you don't know anything about it. I read in *FanzMag* that Johnny Buck likes girls who are outgoing, bold, and have a good sense of humor. I'd say that's me."

Steven took a bite of cereal and snorted disdainfully.

"Jessica *is* outgoing and bold. Plus, she definitely knows how to have a good time," Elizabeth said, taking up for Jessica. "Johnny Buck might be a little old for her but . . ."

"A *little?*" Steven squeaked.

"You don't know anything about Johnny Buck or me," Jessica shouted angrily.

"That's enough!" Mr. Wakefield said curtly, coming into the kitchen with his briefcase. "Steven, stop teasing your sister. Jessica, stop being so silly. It's fine for you to meet Johnny Buck, but try to be sensible. You're too young to be thinking about anybody seriously, much less someone like Johnny Buck."

Jessica dropped her eyes and pushed her cereal around in her bowl. Typical Steven—trying to rain on her parade. He was like Lila. He just couldn't stand it that something so wonderful and glamorous was happening to her and not him.

Steven was being a jerk, but she wasn't going to let him get to her, she decided. Life was going too well to sulk. She lifted her face and smiled sunnily at Elizabeth. "So how do you think they'll officially notify me that I'm the contest winner? Johnny said, 'I'll be in touch.' Think he'll call me personally?"

"Why do you have to be notified," Steven asked. "You know already."

"Yeah, but Johnny Buck doesn't know that," Jessica pointed out. "I mean, he doesn't know that I was watching TV the other day. I might have been out riding, or driving my convertible along the beach, or something like that."

"You don't have a convertible," Steven said damply. "You don't even have a driver's license."

Jessica rolled her eyes. He was so dense. "*Johnny*

Buck doesn't know that," Jessica repeated impatiently. "He doesn't know anything about me, so somebody will have to officially notify me. See? How else would I know what time to meet him and stuff like that?"

"Jessica's right," Elizabeth said. "But I doubt Johnny Buck will call you himself. It'll probably be somebody who works for him or for *Sweet Talk.*"

Jessica snapped her fingers. "Maybe a big white limousine will drive up with a life-sized poster of Johnny Buck on the roof. One of Johnny's people will get out and deliver the news with a hundred balloons and a crate of autographed Johnny Buck CDs."

"You are planning to share, I hope," Elizabeth said with a smile.

"Only the balloons and CDs," Jessica answered flirtatiously. "But Johnny is all mine."

"Jessica!" Mrs. Wakefield scolded, coming into the kitchen just in time to hear the last part of the conversation. "You're going to have to cool it or we're not going to let you meet this boy at all."

"Ha!" Steven blurted.

Jessica stuck out her tongue at him, then exchanged a smile with Elizabeth.

"When do you think they'll contact you?" Elizabeth asked.

"Today, I guess. I mean, they'd have to. The concert is only a few days away." Jessica wiggled her toes happily under the table. She hoped the limo would show up at school so that everybody would see—particularly Lila.

"Maybe they'll drop a leaflet from a hot-air balloon," Elizabeth suggested. "Remember when Johnny had a love letter delivered that way in his *Soaring Hearts* video? It was so romantic."

"Wouldn't that be cool?" Jessica breathed. "Lila would just die!"

"They'd have to get permission from the Federal Aviation Bureau," Steven said. "I seriously doubt they'll do that just to tell you that you won some dumb contest."

"I don't care what you think," Jessica said haughtily. "All I know is that whatever Johnny Buck does, it's first class all the way. So there!"

Jessica tossed her hair off of her shoulders and pushed back her seat. "I'm going to brush my teeth. If anybody arrives with, say, two dozen roses and a handwritten note from Johnny, you can find me upstairs. Oh my gosh!" she cried, her stomach sinking.

"What's the matter?" Elizabeth asked her.

"I just realized—they'll probably send a photographer. I mean, they'll want to get my reaction to the good news, won't they?"

"You've already gotten the good news," Steven said. "They missed your reaction."

"They don't know that, you idiot! How many times do I have to tell you?" Jessica bellowed at the top of her voice.

"Jessica!" Mr. and Mrs. Wakefield both said sharply at the same time.

"Apologize to your brother for that rude tone," Mr. Wakefield said sternly.

Jessica was in too much of a hurry to defend herself. Even though the argument was totally Steven's fault, she mumbled a quick (and completely insincere) apology and raced out of the kitchen.

She ran upstairs to her room, determined to change into something more photogenic. Jessica wasn't the neat half of the Wakefield twins, so most of her wardrobe was scattered on the floor and over the end of her bed.

After a few seconds of frantic digging, Jessica found what she'd been looking for—a red silk T-shirt and a black flounced miniskirt. The outfit looked great with her chunky black sandals.

The ensemble was kind of dressy for a regular school day, but this day wasn't going to be regular by any means. Jessica quickly changed her clothes and went into the bathroom to check her face. Most of the Unicorns didn't wear makeup unless it was a special occasion. But what occasion could be more special than today?

Jessica felt a fluttering sensation between her shoulder blades. Her breath came in shallow gulps. Soon she would be meeting Johnny Buck in person. If not today, then next Saturday.

Her feelings for him were so strong, it was just

impossible that he wouldn't feel the same way about her. It would be love at first sight.

Sure there was a slight age difference, but in a few years, it wouldn't matter at all. And in the meantime, they could be the closest of friends— maybe even singing partners.

She closed her eyes, picturing herself onstage with Johnny Buck. They wore matching shirts and swayed to the driving beat of a song they had written together.

They held the last note until the crowd began to applaud. Finally the song was over and the audience jumped to its feet. Jessica could see Lila, Rachel, Ellen, Mandy, and Kimberly in the front row watching her.

"I always knew Jessica was an incredibly talented and wonderful person," Rachel said to the other girls. "And for sure more talented and wonderful than Lila. No wonder Johnny Buck picked her to be his best gal pal and singing partner."

"Jessica!" Elizabeth shouted from downstairs.

Jessica quickly dabbed a little gloss on her lips and brushed some color on her cheeks. Her fingers shook with excitement. Maybe the notification had arrived. She ran out of the bathroom, through her room, and came to a skidding stop at the top of the stairs. "Are they here?" she gasped.

Elizabeth looked up at her from the bottom of the stairs. "No. But we're going to be late if we don't get going."

Jessica rolled her eyes. "How can you worry about mundane stuff like being late for school on a day like today?"

Steven came barreling out of his room zipping his backpack. "Even contest winners have to go to school," he said, thumping down the stairs. "If I were you, I wouldn't wait for your principal to officially inform you about that. You might wind up grounded."

He's just jealous, Jessica told herself.

"What are you looking at?" Mandy asked, pulling her denim slouch hat farther down over her brow. Every few minutes Jessica squinted up at the sky as if she'd just discovered a new comet or something. It was starting to make Mandy nervous.

"I'm waiting for official notification that I won the contest," Jessica answered.

Mandy giggled. "Are you expecting a carrier pigeon?"

Jessica grinned. "No. But maybe a hot-air balloon."

Mandy smiled. "Whatever happens, I'm sure it will be exciting. But right now, I'm more excited about lunch. Come on. Let's go eat. I'm starving."

"I can't think about food at a time like this," Jessica protested.

"Then come to the cafeteria and watch me eat," Mandy responded.

"I'll come. But not to witness your exciting

cafeteria experience. I want to watch Lila eat her heart out."

Mandy quickened her steps. She and Jessica left the main hallway and entered the bright and sunny school cafeteria. The other Unicorns were already sitting at their private table they called the "Unicorner."

Lila waved them over and Mandy and Jessica hurriedly took their seats. "Gosh, Jessica," Lila said. "You look as if you didn't sleep very well. You've got big bags under your eyes."

Jessica immediately looked alarmed. She reached into her purse and found a small compact.

Mandy smothered a giggle. It was obvious that Lila was just trying to bug Jessica. Jessica and Lila were really competitive and Lila was probably greener than grass over Jessica winning the contest.

While Jessica patted her eye area, trying to find signs of bagging, Mandy noticed the other girls exchanging glances. She felt a tingle of suspicion. Something was up. She could tell. She raised her eyebrows questioningly at Kimberly.

Kimberly responded to Mandy's eyebrow query by clearing her throat. "Jessica, we've been having a little informal meeting before you and Mandy got here."

"Uh-huh," Jessica murmured absently, holding the mirror far away so that she could see her whole face at once.

"We've been talking about how being in a club

means sharing—sharing good times and bad."

Jessica closed her compact with a suspicious snap. She glanced around the table. "What are you getting at?"

"We'd like to meet Johnny Buck too," Lila explained sweetly. "As a fellow Unicorn, we think you have a responsibility to include us in your day with him."

"No way!" Jessica squeaked.

"Why not?" Ellen asked.

"Because Johnny and I have something special," Jessica answered.

"Like what?" Ellen pressed.

"You've never even met him," Rachel pointed out.

Jessica shook her head. "It doesn't matter. We have a chemistry. Or at least we will. It's not that I don't love you guys, but this is my dream come true. I'm going to spend the day with Johnny Buck—just the two of us. I've got it all planned."

Mandy leaned forward with the rest of the Unicorns, eager for details. "What are you going to do?" she asked.

"Well, first of all, I'll show him around town. He'll want to see where I go to school and hang out and stuff like that. Then, when he feels as if he really knows me, we'll go for a ride. After that, we'll head for the lake, where we'll wash off the dust. And of course we'll probably sing a few of his tunes together."

Mandy leaned back in her chair and imagined

what it would be like to be onstage with Johnny, looking into his eyes and singing a sweet ballad. Jessica was so lucky.

Ellen let out a sigh. "Unreal! It's like the ultimate dream date."

"That's right," Jessica said, her face falling into stubborn lines. "And a date is for two people—not a club."

"You're wrong," Lila told her. "This is not a date. It's a historic event. Not just for you, but for the whole club. Jessica, this is bigger than just you and Johnny Buck. Think about the Unicorns of the future. Don't you want them to know that a Unicorn won the 'Meet Johnny Buck' contest? And do you really want to keep him all to yourself? Don't you want your friends to see you and Johnny together?"

Jessica chewed a nail. She looked torn. Mandy knew she would be too. She wanted to show off. Who didn't? But on the other hand, she didn't want to share Johnny, and Mandy didn't blame her.

Once the Unicorns started competing for the spotlight and Johnny Buck's attention, Jessica would have to fight hard not to get squeezed out of her own date.

"I have an idea," Lila said, snapping her fingers and sucking in her breath, as if she had just been struck by a thought.

But Mandy wasn't fooled. She'd known Lila a long time. Whatever Lila was about to suggest, it had been on her mind from the very beginning.

"My dad gave me a brand new camcorder last week," Lila began. "What if I followed you and Johnny all day and filmed? It would be sort of like a documentary. Only it would be a 'docudate.' That way, we could all watch it and the event would be preserved for Unicorn posterity."

"Great idea!" Kimberly said. "I'll go with you and make sure the light and sound are just right."

"I'll carry the tripod," Ellen said. "You don't want too much jerky camera motion. Sure it adds realism, but it also gives everybody a headache after a while."

"We could mount the camera on top of my dad's Range Rover," Rachel suggested.

Mandy giggled. It looked as though the whole Unicorn Club would be going along on Jessica's dream date after all.

"Hold it!" Jessica said, lifting her hand. "You guys are getting totally out of control."

"But it's such a superfabulous idea," Lila protested. "Don't you want your friends to see you and Johnny Buck hanging together?"

"I do think it's a good idea," Jessica said. "But I want the right to pick my own director."

The girls fell silent.

"*One* person can come along. But that's it," Jessica said. "And she has to stay in the background."

"As your best friend—and the person who has

the passes—I think it's obvious who should direct," Lila said quickly.

"Trust Lila to try to skunk the rest of us," Rachel said angrily. "Forget the VIP passes. My dad can get us tickets if Lila finks on us. He gave a bundle to the children's hospital. Jessica, you know what a great photo sense I have. Don't you think—since I'm the newest member of the club—it would be a really wonderful gesture on your part to pick me?"

Jessica sat back in her seat. "I like the idea of a docudate. But I want it done right. That means I want the most sensitive, artistic, and creative person in the club."

Mandy's heart began to beat a bit faster. She had a feeling she knew what Jessica was hinting at.

"I want Mandy," Jessica announced.

Mandy caught her breath and clasped her hands over her chest. This was fantastic. She'd tried hard not to be jealous of Jessica, but deep down she was.

Mandy really wanted to meet Johnny Buck and get to know him—but not for the same reason as the other girls. She thought he was cute and talented and all that. But she admired him mostly for what he was doing for the children's hospital.

Mandy had had cancer the year before. She had been treated at the Sweet Valley Children's Hospital. Without the dedication and talent of the staff there, she wouldn't be here today. Anybody who donated their time and talent to the hospital was high on Mandy's list of personal heroes. "I accept," she said quietly. "And I promise to do the very best job of documenting the experience that I can." Mandy did have a very artistic sense. She had always hoped to direct something someday, and here was a project she could really believe in.

"I think we should start this afternoon," Jessica said.

"What happens this afternoon?" Kimberly asked.

"I'm sure that the contest people will notify me in some really big way that I'm the winner," Jessica answered. "It'll make a great opening scene for the video."

Mandy sat back and smiled, already picturing the way she would shoot the scene. Her docudate would be a true and honest portrayal of a star and his fan.

Three

Jessica sat on the front steps of the Wakefield house and stared dreamily into the distance.

"That's good," Mandy said. "That's good. Hold that pose. Now, tell me how you're feeling while you wait for the big news."

Jessica frowned. "Wait a minute. I want to act surprised when they get here. Like I don't know that I'm the winner."

Mandy shook her head. "This is a docudate. That means it's the truth. The truth is that you know you won."

"Yeah. But it'll be much more dramatic if I'm just sitting here. Then, when this big car pulls up and a guy gets out carrying balloons and a huge poster of Johnny Buck, I'll do something like this. . . ." Jessica jumped up, placed her hands on either side of her cheeks in surprise, and gasped. "You mean . . . I won? . . . I'm going to meet Johnny Buck?" Jessica let her head fall back. She opened her arms wide and spun in a circle. "It's a dream come true," she gushed.

Mandy rolled her eyes. "That looks totally phony. I don't believe it for a minute. Let's just do this the way they do it in real documentaries."

Jessica put her hands on her hips. "Mandy! This is the biggest thing that's ever happened in my whole life. I want it to be big and dramatic. Romantic even."

Before they could continue their argument, they heard the sound of an engine—a large engine. Both girls looked toward the corner. A long white car was coming around the corner. A limo!

"It's them," Jessica squeaked. "It's them. It has to be."

Mandy hoisted the camera. "Just forget I'm here," she advised. "Just let things happen."

Jessica ran to the curb. The limo was getting closer and closer. As it neared the house, Mandy suddenly heard the sound of cheering.

She turned around and saw Lila, Rachel, Ellen, and Kimberly running out from behind the neighbors' hedge. They held up a huge banner that said, "Sweet Valley Loves Johnny Buck!" Screaming with excitement, they ran into the street, stretching the banner across it.

The limo slowed down.

"Get away!" Jessica shouted angrily. "You'll ruin everything."

But the Unicorns ignored her. They waved their arms and shook the banner, jumping up and down.

Mandy ran to the sidewalk with her camera. As a friend, she felt sorry for Jessica. Having the Unicorns horn in on her big moment was pretty hard. As a director, though, Mandy was thrilled by this spontaneous and unplanned surprise. A real-life drama was unfolding right in front of her—and she was there to get it on tape. It was a great scene full of conflict with a capital *C*.

Mandy could see how directors might become callous. She knew Jessica was unhappy, but right now she was more interested in capturing the story than she was in Jessica's feelings.

Mandy aimed her camera and panned the group, trying to get each expression: Jessica's resentful scowl; Kimberly's hopeful smile; Ellen's goofy, close-to-tears, upside-down grin; Rachel's wide-eyed, thrilled-with-life smile; Lila's slack-jawed, red-faced look of embarrassment.

Look of embarrassment? That didn't make sense. Mandy backed up and closed in on Lila. Why did Lila look embarrassed?

The limo came to a stop and the driver got out. He stared at the girls in wonder and scratched his head in bewilderment. "Ms. Fowler?" the driver finally said. "Is that you?"

Lila groaned and dropped her end of the banner. "Shaw! What are you doing here?"

"Lila! That's *your* car!" Ellen exclaimed.

"Duh!" Lila snapped.

"But that's not your chauffeur," Ellen pointed out.

"Our regular chauffeur is on vacation. Shaw is filling in," Lila explained. She stared irritably at the man. "What are you doing here?"

Shaw gestured over his shoulder with his thumb and grinned.

"I just had the car serviced at the garage on the corner. There's construction on the main boulevard, so I'm going back to the house through the neighborhood." He chuckled. "Sure was nice of you girls to give me such a big welcome."

"We thought you were someone else," Lila told him. "Sorry. You can go on."

"Can I give you girls a ride somewhere?" he asked, getting in the car.

"Yes!" Jessica said.

"No!" they all answered.

"I'm going back to the estate then. Bye." Shaw waved and drove down the street.

Kimberly and Rachel carefully folded the banner and the group shambled out of the street and back on the sidewalk.

Lila walked up to Mandy and put her hand over the lens, blotting out the picture.

"Hey!" Mandy protested.

"This is stupid," Lila said. "You don't need to film this. We'll look like dorks."

"You deserve to look like dorks," Jessica said angrily.

"Now go home. I want to look surprised when Johnny's people come with the news."

Mandy lowered the camera. "I told you, Jessica. A documentary is supposed to be the truth."

Jessica's face was stubborn. Mandy realized she was going to have to baby her "star" a little. She put her arm over Jessica's shoulder and walked her a few feet away from the others.

"Jessica, it's not as if this is the date. Johnny Buck won't be here. And I really think that having your friends with you will leave a much clearer picture for posterity of who Jessica Wakefield was. She wasn't a loner with no friends to celebrate with her. She was a popular girl. A member of the Unicorns. A person who naturally attracted attention."

Mandy wondered if she had gone just a teensy-weensy bit over the top. But when she saw Jessica's starry-eyed, rapt look, she realized Jessica had bought it.

"You're right," Jessica said. "I want the generations of Unicorns to come to see that Jessica Wakefield was a popular girl with lots of friends *who were very jealous of her.*"

Mandy smiled and adjusted the bill of her baseball cap. "All right! Then let's get back to it." She looked over to where the Unicorns stood in a dispirited clump, waiting for their decision.

"You can stay," Mandy told them.

"Yea!" The Unicorns came to life and cheered.

"Here comes another car!" Kimberly shouted. "Get ready. Get ready." She and Ellen unfolded the banner. The group stretched it along the sidewalk this time instead of across the street.

Mandy lifted the video camera and began to film.

But the approaching car wasn't a limo. It was Mr. Wakefield's sedan. He smiled and waved as he turned into the driveway.

The girls groaned and Mandy sighed. At this rate, she would be out of film by the time the contest officials arrived. And the Unicorns would be out of energy.

"Yeaaaaa, Johnny Buck!" Ellen screamed. She jumped up and ran to the curb as a car came around the corner.

It was a sports car, and it barely slowed as it passed the house.

Jessica sat on the front steps with the other Unicorns, watching glumly as Ellen came trudging back.

At this point, Ellen was the only Unicorn with enough energy and enthusiasm to greet every passing car in hope that it was a contest official bringing big news. Even Mandy had stopped filming.

Lila looked at her watch. "It's five o'clock. Let's go home. If they haven't come by now, they're not going to."

"We'll meet back here tomorrow," Rachel said. "I heard Johnny Buck tell Jessica he would be in touch, and I want to be here when it happens."

Jessica was grateful that Rachel was still so enthused. Even Jessica herself was beginning to feel doubtful. Maybe it had all been a mistake. Maybe they had decided she wasn't the winner after all. Maybe nobody was going to come and make a big fuss over her or bring her balloons or anything like that.

It would be horrible! Not just for her, but for everybody in the club—not to mention the generations of Unicorns yet to come.

"Is it okay if we come back tomorrow?" Ellen asked.

Jessica lifted her chin and pretended to think it over. But really and truly, she *wanted* them to come back. If tomorrow was anything like today, she for sure didn't want to sit outside waiting by herself. She wanted company.

"Well," she said, as if she were granting them a huge favor. "I know that whatever Johnny Buck does is going to be fabulous and impressive, and I wouldn't want you to miss it. So yes, I guess you guys can come back."

Kimberly stood up and dusted off the seat of her jeans. "I've got to go home. I'm supposed to help with dinner tonight."

"I've got to go home too," Ellen said. "My mom said I have to start my homework earlier so I don't stay up as late."

One after the other, her friends drifted off, and pretty soon, Jessica was alone on the front steps. She couldn't resist taking one last look at the sky to see if she saw a multicolored hot-air balloon winding its way toward her.

But there was nothing in the sky except a late afternoon chill.

Four

"Maybe it was all a mistake," Ellen said nervously.

"Stop saying that," Mandy begged, searching through her locker for her math textbook. "It can't be a mistake. Everybody heard the show. Johnny Buck looked right into the camera and said Jessica's name."

"It seems as if somebody from the record company or the TV show would have gotten in touch by now." Rick Hunter slammed his locker closed. "It's been two days and the concert is this Saturday."

Lila sat on a bench beside the locker bank, lacing up her new boots. "I'll bet it's all a big nothing," she said with a sniff.

"What do you mean?" Mandy asked.

Lila shrugged and pulled down her mouth in a very cynical way. "It was probably just a publicity stunt. They're not really going to deliver on what they promised. We were stupid to think it would really happen. Why should a big star like Johnny Buck take time out of his schedule to meet Jessica?"

Ellen scratched her ankle with the toe of her other foot. "You mean the contest was phony?"

"It could be. My dad says most contests are come-ons," Aaron Dallas said. "It sure seems suspicious that nobody's gotten in touch with Jessica to follow up."

Mandy felt her face fall. Maybe they were right. It was sure starting to look that way. Deep disappointment made Mandy's stomach feel as if she'd eaten a lead weight for breakfast. She didn't want to think that Johnny Buck had just used them to promote the concert. Surely he knew it was important to follow through? Any fan who took the trouble to enter the contest would care very much about getting to meet Johnny and show him around Sweet Valley. Most of the kids who lived here were pretty proud of their town.

"I think I'll get my camcorder back from you this afternoon if you don't mind," Lila said to Mandy.

"Let's just wait one more day," Mandy begged. "I'm sure the contest is for real. Maybe he's busy getting ready for the concert. Maybe he lost Jessica's name and address."

"Maybe he just doesn't care about meeting Jessica," Lila said. "I mean, after all, who are the

Wakefields? If Rachel or I had won, those contest officials would have been here by now with a big brass band."

Mandy saw Jessica come around the corner and stop short in her tracks. It was evident by the crimson blush rising on her cheeks that she had appeared just in time to hear Lila's little speech.

"Oh yeah?" Jessica blurted.

"Yeah," Lila answered casually. "I'm sure that Johnny Buck's people and the *Sweet Talk* TV show know who's who around Sweet Valley. Nobody's ever heard of you and—"

"You are just totally jealous," Jessica snapped, cutting her off. "And you don't know anything about it. I'm sick of your attitude. From now on, the Unicorn Club is barred from participating in my docudate. So don't bother coming over this afternoon."

"Don't worry," Lila snapped. "We won't."

Lila and Jessica stalked off in opposite directions. Mandy closed her locker. Lila hadn't said anything else about the camcorder and Mandy wasn't going to remind her. *One more day*, she told herself. *Just give him one more day.*

"I told you," Steven said to Jessica at home that afternoon. "They probably figure you know already so they're not going to bother with an official notification."

Elizabeth nodded. "He's right. Relax. Johnny

Buck'll probably ring the doorbell on the day of the concert and whisk you off in his limo."

"I hope so," Jessica said nervously. "But what if he forgot? Maybe I should call the TV station."

Mrs. Wakefield came walking through the living room shuffling a handful of mail. "Elizabeth, here's your *Teen Editor* magazine. Steven, you got something from your coach. Looks like the game schedule for next semester. Jessica, here's a postcard for you."

Jessica took the postcard. It didn't have a picture on it or anything. It was just a plain yellow paper card addressed to . . . "Wakefield, J." in computer-generated type. She turned it over and read:

Dear Contest Winner,
    Please call the number below for details.

"This is it!" Jessica jumped to her feet and thundered to the telephone in the hall. "I'm supposed to call for details," she told the others breathlessly. "Maybe they want to be sure I'm home before they send out the limo and photographer."

Steven and Elizabeth gathered around her, watching as she punched in the number. Jessica tried to compose her voice as the phone rang. "I wonder who I'll talk to," she said. "Maybe it'll be Bobby Carroway."

"Operator 346," a bored woman said, answering the phone on the fourth ring.

"Hello? This is Jessica Wakefield calling." Jessica's voice came out high, thin, and very young sounding.

She took a deep breath, determined to drop her voice to a more mature octave. "I'm calling about the contest."

Steven and Elizabeth pressed in closer, so that they could listen along with Jessica.

"Which contest?" the woman asked.

Jessica blinked in confusion. "There's more than one?"

The woman let out an impatient breath. "This is Digital Net. We're a subcontracted service provider for AGS&C, Inc."

Jessica shot a look at Steven. *What* was the woman talking about? Steven shook his head. "I'm sorry," Jessica said. "I don't understand. What is AGS&C?"

"American Games, Sweepstakes, and Contests, Incorporated."

"Are you in Hollywood?" Jessica asked.

"We're in Upton, Minnesota."

"What is Johnny Buck doing in Minnesota?" Jessica asked, feeling utterly bewildered.

"Who?" the woman asked.

"Johnny Buck. I'm the winner of the 'Meet Johnny Buck' contest," Jessica explained.

"Did you receive a yellow postcard from us?" Operator 346 asked.

"Yes. That's where I got your phone number."

"What is your contestant number?"

"My what?"

"Your contestant number. It's in the upper right-hand corner. A computer code starting with two zeros."

Jessica saw the number. It was half faded and hard to read. "It looks like 0078542367891."

"One moment while I transfer your call," the operator said, putting Jessica on hold.

Jessica listened to the whir and whoosh of Minnesota's deep telephone space. The line rang several times, clicked, and then suddenly the familiar strains of "Messenger of Love" came blasting through the telephone line.

Jessica smiled. "Now we're getting somewhere," she told Steven and Elizabeth. They pressed in a little closer.

The music ended and a loud recorded voice boomed in Jessica's ear. "Welcome to the 'Meet Johnny Buck' line. An operator will be with you shortly. But while you wait, listen to this list of CDs and merchandise available for purchase at a music store in your area. *Johnny Buck Rocks*, the Grammy-winning video, is on sale this month only for twenty percent off with proof of purchase of any new Johnny Buck CD. Just bring your sales receipt and packaging with visible bar code to . . ."

"I don't believe this!" Steven sputtered. "They're actually making you listen to a commercial for Johnny Buck stuff. Talk about pushy."

"Shhh!" Jessica frowned. It seemed weird to her too, but she wasn't going to let anybody criticize Johnny Buck around her. "The proceeds probably go to charity or something."

Finally a human voice answered. "Meet Johnny

Buck, how can I help you?"

"This is Jessica Wakefield. I'm the contest winner and I'm trying to find out what I'm supposed to do."

"May I have your contestant number, please?"

Jessica read off the long number again. She heard the tap, tap, tapping of computer keys on the other end of the phone. "Okay. I've found the information. According to the advertised terms of the contest, Johnny Buck will come to your home at 10:30 A.M. next Saturday for a photo session."

Elizabeth pumped her fist victoriously.

"Will you be talking to him before then?" Jessica asked.

"To who?"

"Johnny Buck!" Jessica rolled her eyes.

"I'm sorry. I do not know Mr. Buck personally. We are a telecommunications company in Tredille, Nevada," the lady said.

Jessica wondered if she was having a dream. "But the other lady said you were in Minnesota."

"Digital Net is in Minnesota. We're in Nevada."

"Who are you?"

"Amalgamated National Telephone Response Corporation," the woman answered.

Jessica closed her eyes and groaned. "I don't have any idea what you're talking about. But are you sure Johnny Buck is going to be coming to my house Saturday morning?"

"According to Section 409 of the Games and Sweepstakes Code, all prizes must be awarded in accordance with the advertised terms of the contest."

"Is that a yes?" Jessica inquired feebly.

Mandy rang Jessica's doorbell. She was late today, and after Jessica's earlier blowup in the hall, she wasn't sure if she was wanted. But she had hoped that even though Jessica was mad about her friends' lack of faith in Johnny, she would still want everything that *did* happen filmed.

When Jessica opened the door, her slightly dazed expression made Mandy's heart skip a beat. "Something happened," she said. "Am I right?"

Jessica opened and closed her mouth a few times as if she were in shock.

Mandy took her arm and shook it. "What's going on? Tell me."

"You said you didn't want any rehearsed or pre-planned moments, so I don't want to ruin the surprise," Jessica said.

Mandy drew in her breath. "You heard?"

Jessica looked furtively out the door as if she expected to see the Unicorns lurking somewhere. "I'm not really at liberty to say. There are very strict rules about contests and stuff. They've got a code and everything. But for historical purposes, I just feel as if I have a duty to let you know that . . . well . . . an event of historical importance is about to take place."

Mandy's heart began to beat faster and her shoulders sagged with relief. She'd begun to lose her faith in Johnny Buck. Thinking that he might have welched out had made her feel totally depressed.

"Can you tell me when, exactly?" Mandy asked.

"Ummmm . . . not right now," Jessica said. "All I can tell you is that something special is going to happen—and it's going to happen tomorrow. Now I gotta go," she said. "See you at school."

With that, Jessica shut the door. Mandy heard it lock.

Wow! Jessica was really taking this seriously. Usually the girl couldn't keep a secret for two minutes. Mandy turned and started down the walk. She was going to have a hard time sleeping tonight. There were so many things to think about and plan.

Mandy lifted the camera and filmed the house. "Meet Johnny Buck," she said dramatically. "The story begins."

"Give me one good reason why I should help you," Steven challenged an hour later.

"Because you're my brother and you don't want me to be unhappy," Jessica said.

Steven made a face as though he wasn't quite sure that was true.

"Because I'll make it worth your while," Jessica added. "I'll do your chores for a week."

"Two weeks," Steven countered.

Jessica was desperate enough to agree to three weeks, but she didn't want Steven to know that. "Okay," she agreed. "Two weeks."

"What do I have to do?" Steven asked.

Jessica held up a large card on which she had carefully lettered the words:

"Meet Me in the Front Yard" at 10:30 A.M.
on Saturday.

Love,
Johnny

She had written the song title in gold ink on a blue background. "Help me find somebody to deliver this with a big bunch of balloons."

"Why?"

"Because everybody expects me to be notified in a really big way. If I tell them I just got a crummy postcard and an operator in Nevada, they'll just think the whole thing is a big nothing. They'll think I'm a big nothing."

"Why can't I just deliver the card?"

"Because all my friends know you," Jessica explained.

"So we're just going to get some guy off the street?" Steven looked at Jessica as if she had lost her mind. "That's crazy."

"No. We're going to the Sweet Valley Musicians Hall. There are a lot of cool-looking people down there and musicians are always looking for work. We'll find just the right person and hire him to pretend he's delivering a message from Johnny. Please, Steven! Please!"

"Okay, okay," Steven agreed in a grudging tone.

"But not because you're going to do my chores. But because if I say no, you'll go do it anyway. And if you go by yourself, and Mom and Dad find out about it, they'll kill me and ground us both for the rest of our lives."

Jessica grinned. "All right! Let's go now before it closes." She put the card in her backpack and hurried outside. Her bike leaned against the side of the house.

"Forget the bike," Steven said. "We'll go on the moped."

"Cool!" Jessica said. "You got it to work?"

"Yeah," Steven told her proudly. "It took me and Joe Howell a solid week to find the problem, but it's running smoothly now."

Steven's moped was his pride and joy. He'd saved up for months to buy it. It was only slightly used, and he and Joe Howell, his best friend, had painted it a bright, shiny red.

Steven got the moped out of the garage, and he and Jessica both put on helmets. She climbed on the seat behind him and pretty soon they were entering the area of downtown Sweet Valley where the music clubs and discos were located.

A charming two-story brick building on the corner of one of the town's oldest blocks served as the Musicians Hall. Jessica and Steven pulled up to the front and got off the moped.

Three old men sat on a bench in front of the building, chatting and laughing. Two of them wore berets and one wore a cowboy hat.

An elderly woman and another man came out the front door. The man carried a guitar case and walked with a cane. The woman carried a large bass.

"This looks more like an old folks home than a cool hangout," Steven said under his breath.

Jessica looked up and down the street. Steven was right. She didn't see any cool-looking young men or women anywhere around. Then she spotted a big black motorcycle parked by the curb. "I wonder who that belongs to?" she said, nudging Steven's arm.

The front door opened again. This time, a tall, good-looking guy around eighteen years old came out wearing a leather jacket and jeans. He carried a motorcycle helmet under his arm and hurried to assist the lady struggling under the weight of the bass. "Here. Let me carry that to your car," he offered.

"That guy would be perfect," Jessica exclaimed. "He even looks like Johnny Buck."

The young man helped the woman load the instrument into the trunk. Then he assisted the man with the cane.

"It was so nice to meet you," the woman told him as she got into the front seat with her companion. "I hope you'll jam with us again."

"Thanks for letting me sit in," the young man said. He waved at the car as it pulled away from the curb, then walked over to the motorcycle.

Jessica started forward. "Excuse me!"

The young man turned around and looked at Steven and Jessica. He gave them a friendly but curious smile. "Yes?"

"Are you a musician?" Jessica asked.

"It depends on who you ask," the young man answered with a laugh.

"You must be or you wouldn't be here," Jessica insisted.

"Some of the best retired jazz musicians in the country play together here once a month. If I'm in the area, I like to come by and listen. If I'm lucky, they let me sit in."

"What do you play?" Steven asked.

"Jazz guitar," he answered.

"Would you be interested in a paid gig?" Steven asked.

The young man looked amused. "It depends. What did you have in mind?"

"Actually it doesn't have anything to do with music," Jessica began.

The young man leaned against his motorcycle and cocked his head. "I'm all ears."

Five

Mandy hurried down the hall with her backpack. She'd asked Jessica all day what to expect, but Jessica had refused to tell her.

"Mandy! Wait up!"

Mandy turned and saw Jessica running down the hall to catch up with her.

"Got the camera?" Jessica asked nervously.

"In my locker," Mandy said. "But Lila's been bugging me all day about giving it back. If something doesn't happen soon . . ."

"It will," Jessica promised. "Real soon. Come on."

"I know you can't give me the details. And as you know, I'm totally committed to trying to preserve the integrity of the documentary process. But for historical purposes, I'm willing to ask— where is the best place for me to be in order to capture Unicorn history in the making?"

"On the front steps right after last period," Jessica answered promptly before hurrying away toward class.

The bell rang, signaling that class was about to start. Mandy hurried to history class and took a seat behind Lila.

Her director's instincts began to kick in. She didn't know what exactly was going to happen, but she knew that without reaction shots the film would lose a lot of dramatic impact.

That meant she needed everybody out front—reacting in a big way. On the other hand, she didn't want to give the surprise away by telling them to be out front for the big notification scene. She was going to have to be slightly sneaky.

"Lila," she whispered. "I want to be sure I didn't mess up the zoom for you. How about meeting me on the front steps after school and letting me take a few shots of you? That way I can be sure it's focusing right. And maybe you could say a few words about how you feel about Johnny Buck and the benefit. We want *something* to show for all our trouble."

Lila preened a little. "Sure. I'd be happy to."

"Why don't you get a shot of both of us?" Rachel suggested.

"How about a shot of everybody," Mandy said. "We'll call it *A Unicorn Moment*."

"That's a great idea," Rachel said with a smile.

"It's a terrible idea," Lila snapped.

"How come?" Rachel demanded.

"Because it's my camcorder," Lila answered.

Rachel shrugged and narrowed her eyes. "Your technology monopoly is over, Fowler. I've got a video camera too. If you don't let Mandy tape all of us with *your* camera, I'll let her use my camera. And we'll leave *you* out."

Lila rolled her eyes. "Oh, all right! But I really don't see why we all have to be in the picture when I'm the one with the VIP passes."

The teacher called the class to order and Mandy sat back in her seat. She fidgeted impatiently with her pencil and notebook while the teacher droned on and on about the War of 1812. Usually Mandy was interested in studying history.

Today, though, she was interested in making history.

Jessica stood behind Mandy and looked up and down the street. Where *was* he? Surely he hadn't forgotten about their deal and skipped town? He had seemed so nice.

"Of course, being the child of one of the richest and most influential men in the county isn't always easy," Lila was saying to the video camera.

The rest of the Unicorns stood behind Lila, jostling with one another for a position in front of the camera.

Kimberly rolled her eyes and pretended to play a tiny violin. Rick Hunter, Aaron Dallas, and a few other kids stood off to the side, watching Mandy film.

Aaron Dallas laughed at Kimberly. Ellen, eager to get into the action herself, followed up by forking her fingers over Lila's head like devil horns.

Rick Hunter let out a shout of laughter. Lila shot him a quelling look and composed her face into its most dignified expression.

"The pressures are overwhelming sometimes," Lila went on to say. "People always expect me to wear the latest fashions and have all the newest CDs and electronic equipment."

"Boo hoo!" Rick Hunter pretended to burst out crying.

"Okay, that does it," Lila said angrily. "I'm trying to share an honest moment for posterity and you guys are just ruining it. I'm going home."

Lila walked over and plucked her backpack off the concrete bench.

"Don't go!" Jessica begged. She turned to the audience. "Stop making fun of Lila while she spills her guts."

"I'm going to spill my lunch," Rick chuckled. "Ohhhhh, the pressure of being a spoiled rich girl," he said in a high, teary falsetto.

Aaron responded with a loud crack of laughter.

Rick grinned at his buddy and waved at the group. "I'm out of here, crew. I've got soccer practice."

"I've got basketball practice," Maria announced, picking up her purse and books off the grass. "See you guys later."

"As much as I enjoy listening to Lila complain about being rich, I've got to get going too," Ellen said.

Lots of people laughed. But Jessica felt like crying. The crowd was breaking up and her "Messenger of Love" was a no-show.

"I thought you said something important was going to happen!" Mandy whispered.

Jessica swallowed the lump in her throat. "I thought it was." A tear began to roll down her cheek. "I thought—" She broke off suddenly. "Do you hear that?" she said, putting a hand to her ear.

In the distance she heard a roar. Was it the engine of a motorcycle? The sound got louder and the aggressive buzzing grew closer.

It *was* a motorcycle! And it was coming this way. *Hurry*, she urged mentally. *Hurry.*

Lila was giving Rick Hunter a last piece of her mind. Ellen and Rachel were debating whether to go to the library or to the soda shop. And Kimberly was talking to Aaron about the soccer schedule.

Suddenly a big black motorcycle came roaring around the corner with about a hundred helium balloons attached to the handle.

Every face turned toward the motorcycle at the same time.

"Oh my gosh!" Ellen gasped. "It's . . . it's . . ."

The guy on the motorcycle wore a helmet with the visor down and a leather jacket. He really looked as if he could be Johnny Buck.

The motorcycle roared to a stop.

"Is it Johnny Buck?" Aaron Dallas asked, his mouth falling open.

"No, I'm afraid not." The guy lifted his visor to reveal his handsome face and smile. "I'm the 'Messenger of Love' and I'm looking for Jessica Wakefield."

His eyes searched the crowd and rested on Jessica. "You must be the one. Johnny told me to look for a beautiful blonde with an outgoing, bold personality."

Jessica pretended to be as surprised and awestruck as the others. "You're right. I am Jessica," she said in a fake, trembling voice. She hoped Mandy was getting all this on tape. It was great stuff.

The "Messenger of Love" reached inside his jacket and pulled out the card Jessica had lettered. "I've got a message for you from Johnny Buck."

He detached the balloons from the handle of his motorcycle and presented them and the card to Jessica with a flourish. "My work here is done," he said dramatically. "The rest is up to Johnny Buck, Jessica Wakefield, and . . . *destiny.*" He kicked the motorcycle into gear and let it roar. "Farewell!"

The motorcycle lurched forward and the "Messenger of Love" disappeared around the corner.

The girls surged to the curb, watching him disappear. Then they turned to Jessica.

"What does it say?" Rachel demanded.

Jessica turned toward Mandy and the camera

and held up the card. "It says, 'Meet Me in the Front Yard at 10:30 A.M. on Saturday. Love, Johnny.' "

"How romantic!" Ellen sighed.

"Totally and utterly cool," Rachel agreed.

"Still think Johnny's not interested in meeting me?" Jessica couldn't help asking Lila.

Lila frowned and shrugged. "If he was so interested, how come he didn't come by and notify you himself?"

Jessica opened and closed her mouth, unable to think of a suitably squelching comeback. She noticed all the other kids watching her.

"Yeah, Jessica," Rick echoed. "Now that Lila mentions it, isn't it kind of cheesy to send a Johnny Buck look-alike on a motorcycle?"

A discontented murmur floated through the crowd.

Jessica began to sweat. Trust Lila to take the biggest thing in Jessica's whole life and try to make it seem second-rate and unimportant.

Lila smirked and it made Jessica just furious. Whatever it took, Jessica was going to wipe that haughty look off Lila's face once and for all. She was going to have the most fabulous dream date of the century and she was going to make Lila Fowler's VIP passes look like VSP passes (very small potatoes).

"Actually," Jessica said, "I wasn't supposed to tell anybody, but Johnny did call me himself."

Ellen gasped. "Johnny Buck called you? On the telephone?"

"He did not," Lila snapped.

"Yes, he did. Didn't he, Mandy?"

Jessica looked into Mandy's surprised face. *Please back me up,* she begged silently.

Mandy felt as if someone had just thrown a glass of cold water on her face.

"Mandy was there yesterday afternoon when he called," Jessica explained. "Johnny told me he was just crushed that he wouldn't be able to come by school himself, but he's busy in the studio. He promised to make it up to me when he got here. And he's really looking forward to seeing Sweet Valley. Right, Mandy?"

Mandy swallowed. Lila lifted one skeptical eyebrow. Every eye in the crowd was on Mandy.

Johnny Buck was their hero. They wanted to think he was a great guy. Nobody wanted to hear that Johnny had been too busy, or too disinterested, to come himself.

Normally Mandy hated lies. And as a documentary director, she felt totally opposed to making anything up.

But she also knew how important morale was in the fight against cancer. People rallied around enthusiasm and dedication. Every single student at Sweet Valley Middle School had bought a ticket or made a donation. How long would their enthusiasm last if they didn't think Johnny Buck shared their commitment?

"That's right," she said, swallowing her principles. "I was there."

Jessica's tense face relaxed.

The crowd groaned in envy and admiration.

"That is so cool!" Ellen breathed. "What was his voice like on the telephone?"

"Just like it is on his records," Jessica said with a smile. "Deep and romantic. Right, Mandy?"

"Right," Mandy croaked.

"I had to," Jessica hissed at Mandy later as they moved through the crowd, waving like celebrities. "You saw the way Lila was trashing Johnny. She was trying to make it look really unimportant. Trying to make our docudate unimportant. I couldn't let her get away with it. I would have looked like a total nothing and so would you."

"I didn't lie because I was worried about looking like a nothing," Mandy said firmly, smiling and returning Maria Slater's thumbs-up sign. "I lied because I thought it was in the best interest of the cause. But don't put me on the spot like that again, okay?"

Jessica held up her hand like a Girl Scout making a promise. "I won't. Unicorn's honor. From here on, it's the truth, the whole truth, and nothing but the truth."

Six

"Stop filming. Stop!" Jessica screeched. "I don't have all my makeup on yet."

"Tough," Mandy said. "I'm going for gritty realism."

Jessica dashed around her messy room searching wildly for her other boot and trying to brush her hair at the same time. She dove into a pile of clothing, socks, shoes, and books and began pawing through the tumble, throwing things this way and that. "Oh, wow! Look at this!"

"What did you find, Jessica?" Mandy asked in her director voice.

"My report on the pyramids."

"How long have you been looking for it?"

"Since fifth grade," Jessica answered, tossing it over her shoulder.

Mandy laughed.

Jessica sat up and cocked her head. There was a rumbling, tumbling sound. "Is that thunder?" she asked fearfully. No way did she want it to rain today. It would ruin everything.

Before Mandy could answer, the Unicorns came barging into Jessica's room. The rumbling sound Jessica had heard wasn't nasty weather—it was the sound of Unicorn feet running up the Wakefields' carpeted staircase.

"Out!" Jessica said immediately. She pointed toward the door.

"Please let us stay," Ellen begged, falling to her knees and pressing her hands together.

"No way," Jessica protested. "I told you guys. One person could come along and that's Mandy."

"We don't want to come along," Rachel said in a pleading tone. "We just want to see him when he gets here."

"I don't want you guys hanging around," Jessica protested. "This is going to be a very special moment for me and Johnny, and I'm sure he doesn't want a bunch of people hanging around watching. Now get lost. He's going to be here any minute."

"I can't believe you're not ready," Kimberly said, looking at her watch. "It's almost eleven. You're just lucky he's late."

"What's keeping him?" Ellen fretted, peering out the window.

Lila plopped down on the edge of Jessica's bed. "You guys are like, so gullible. Johnny Buck's not coming. He probably decided it wasn't convenient, so he's blowing it off."

"For your information, he *can't* blow it off," Jessica told her. "It's against the law."

"Huh?"

"According to Section 409 of the Games and Sweepstakes Code, all prizes must be awarded in accordance with the advertised terms of the contest," Jessica said, repeating what the Amalgamated National Telephone Response Corporation operator had told her.

"How do you know that?" Lila asked, her tone suspicious.

Jessica bit her lip. How did she know that? She didn't want to tell Lila the truth—that some impersonal telephone operator in Minnesota or Nevada or someplace like that had informed her. "My father's a lawyer," she said in a haughty tone.

Pleased at her solution to the problem, Jessica went back to looking for her boot. That ought to keep Lila quiet for a while. She tossed a sneaker over her shoulder.

Clank!

"Hey!" Mandy cried as the sneaker bounced off the camera. "Watch it."

"Sorry about that. Aha!" Jessica found her boot under a pile of dirty jeans and pulled it on. She scrambled to her feet, shook her hair out to make it full, and put her hands on her hips. "What do you think?"

Jessica wore slim black pants and a white T-shirt with a cropped denim vest and black leather boots.

"You look fabulous," Rachel told her. "Like you just stepped out of a magazine."

"You look so good, you could be a model," Ellen echoed.

"A supermodel," Kimberly amended. "Or maybe even a rock star."

Jessica frowned. "Hold it. Since when are you guys so complimentary? I know what you're up to. You're trying to butter me up so I won't kick you out. It's not going to work. Now take a hike."

"*Jessica!*" they all wailed.

"I have a suggestion," Mandy said to Jessica. "How about letting them stay, but they have to hide up here in your room and peek out the window. That way Johnny won't see them and you won't have to worry that they'll come popping out of the hedge again."

"Good idea," Jessica said. "You guys can stay and watch. But don't you dare leave this room. If I catch one of you sneaking into the yard, I'll tell Johnny Buck you're a cooty-carrying fifth-grader."

"All right!" the Unicorns yelled, high-fiving one another.

Jessica faced the camera and gave it her biggest smile. "I'm ready to meet the man of my dreams," she said to the camera, turning her thumb up. "So follow me."

Jessica ran out of her room and down the stairs. Mandy ran after her, filming as Jessica opened the front door and stepped onto the walk. She looked down the street and let out a scream of joy. A long black limousine was moving slowly down the block, pausing in front of every third house as if the driver were checking the street numbers.

Jessica ran to the curb and waved until the glossy limo came to a stop. The windows were dark and mirrored. She couldn't see a thing through them.

Then the doors began to open. People came spilling out of the limo like circus clowns out of a miniature car. Men and women dressed in all kinds of outfits streamed out of the vehicle and onto the yard. None of them was Johnny Buck.

Most of them had cell phones clamped against their ears and were talking rapidly. Nobody even seemed to notice Jessica. Nobody greeted her or said hello or anything.

"No can do," a large man in a dark suit with long hair pulled back in a ponytail was saying into his phone. "We keep one hundred percent of the T-shirt revenue, ninety-eight percent of the food concession, and seventy-five percent of the parking. That's our deal—take it or leave it." He clicked off the phone and ran his eyes over the yard and house. Then his gaze fell on Mandy.

"Over here, Sweetheart." He walked over, put a hand on her shoulder, and marched her toward the front of the car. "I'm Stan Keno, Johnny's manager. We're going to take your picture with Johnny right here in front of the limousine and—"

"But . . . I'm not Jessica," Mandy sputtered.

"I'm Jessica!" Jessica waved her hand to get his attention.

But Mr. Keno wasn't listening. "Burt, bring the camera over here. Connie, see if you can get Metrosound on the phone for me. Bill, tell Rod to unload the equipment at the auditorium and be ready to run a sound check in forty minutes."

"Mr. Keno," Mandy said, tugging at his sleeve. "You've made a mistake."

The man looked at the house, then at the green numbers on the address block in the front yard. "Nope. This is the place. The Wakefield house."

"Yes, but I'm Jessica Wakefield," Jessica said, stepping up and standing right in front of him.

Mr. Keno frowned as if he were having a hard time understanding. Then he smacked his forehead. "Okay. Okay. I get it. You're Jessica Wakefield. And you're . . ." He looked at Mandy.

"I'm the documentarian," Mandy explained.

"The what?"

"I'm going to document the events of the day and . . ."

"I have Metrosound on the phone," the blond woman announced, bringing another cell phone to Mr. Keno.

Mr. Keno took the phone. "Never mind, never mind," he told Mandy, waving his hand as if to shoo her away. "Connie, take the camera."

The blond woman reached over and snatched

the video camera from Mandy's hand.

"Hey!" Mandy protested.

"Sorry. We cannot allow any pictures or recordings of negotiations in progress. That information is considered proprietary by Johnny Buck, Incorporated."

"Pedro!" Mr. Keno said into the phone. "I have to finish a quick PR thing. Head on over to the hotel and I'll meet you there. I think I've got a cosponsor on the 'Johnny Rocks Japan' deal. See you there." He hung up the phone, thrust it at Connie, and then checked his watch. "Okay, Jessica," he said to Mandy.

"I'm Jessica," Jessica protested.

"Whatever," the man said, hurrying to the last door on the back of the limo. He put his hand on the door and smiled at the girls. "Get ready to meet the man."

The door opened and Jessica felt herself tremble from head to toe. This was it. The big moment.

There was a long pause. Jessica couldn't help smiling. Johnny Buck had such a great sense of dramatic timing. She ran her fingers through her hair, giving it a quick tousle.

A long, denim-clad leg emerged from the car. And as Jessica and Mandy watched, the great Johnny Buck stepped out. He wore dark wraparound sunglasses and had a perfect, glowing tan.

Jessica smiled, waiting for him to see her. Her heart thundered. Her knees shook. He seemed to be looking right at her through the glasses. She smiled shyly.

Johnny Buck walked toward her. It was as if somebody had flipped a switch and every other thing in the universe had disappeared. She couldn't hear a thing except the beating of her own heart.

He stretched out his hand and took Jessica's. He whipped off his sunglasses and delivered his killer smile just as the photographer raced up and snapped a picture.

Jessica opened her mouth to speak. There were so many things she wanted to tell him, she hardly knew where to start. "Johnny," she began.

But to her amazement he had already released her hand and turned away, putting his sunglasses back on. He ducked into the back of the limo and suddenly it was as if the scene had been flipped into rewind. The process began to reverse itself.

The people, the cell phones, and the cameras all piled back into the long black vehicle. Connie handed Mandy her video camera and dove into the limo.

"What's going on?" Mandy asked. "Where are they all going?"

Jessica shook her head in bewilderment. "I don't know."

Mr. Keno was talking on the phone again. He paused just long enough to pat Jessica on the head. "We'll send you a copy of the photo just as soon as we have a good print. Watch the paper—it may be in there tomorrow."

"I don't understand," Jessica cried. "You're not leaving, are you?"

"You know how it is. Busy, busy, busy," Mr. Keno said with a smile, waving as he climbed into the car.

Jessica clutched at the door handle. "But you can't leave. I'm supposed to meet Johnny Buck."

Mr. Keno paused as if he were losing patience. "You did meet him."

"No, I didn't. Not really. He didn't even say anything to me," she protested.

Mr. Keno turned and addressed Johnny over the back of the seat. "Johnny, say something to her."

"It was nice to meet you," a slightly squeaky voice in the back responded.

Jessica frowned. That didn't sound much like the Johnny Buck she was used to hearing. She could feel the eyes of the Unicorns staring at the scene through the upstairs blinds.

"Mr. Keno," she said, her voice breaking with desperation. "I told my friends I was going to meet Johnny Buck and show him around town. That's what Bobby Carroway said on *Sweet Talk* and . . ."

Mr. Keno smiled and said, "Jessica, Sweetie Pie, listen, I hear you. I know where you're coming from. And I don't want you to be disappointed, so how about we send you and all your friends a complete set of Johnny Buck CDs along with a T-shirt, autographed photo, and button? It's a one-hundred-dollar value," he added in a serious tone.

"My friends already have his CDs," she cried. The engine started. Jessica cast a frantic look toward

Mandy. "I'm sorry, Jessica," Mr. Keno said, "but we really are pressed for time. The concert is tonight and we've got a million things to take care of. Maybe we'll see you there."

The engine started and Mr. Keno began to roll up the window.

Mandy couldn't believe it. Talk about a gyp! No way was she going to let Mr. Keno get away with this. She pulled Jessica out of the way and pushed her face into the remaining open space of the window. "Excuse me," she said angrily.

"Little girl!" Mr. Keno cried in an alarmed voice. "Be careful. What do you think you're doing?"

"According to Section 409 of the Games and Sweepstakes Code, all prizes must be awarded in accordance with the advertised terms of the contest," Mandy said.

Mr. Keno blinked. "What did you say?"

"I said, according to Section 409 of the Games and Sweepstakes Code, all prizes must be awarded in accordance with the advertised terms of the contest. Bobby Carroway said the winner would get to show Johnny around Sweet Valley. Did Jessica mention her dad is a lawyer, and if she doesn't get to show Johnny Buck around town, she's going to feel a lot of pain and suffer big time?"

There was a long pause while Mr. Keno digested the significance of this piece of information. He and Mandy held a short staring match. Mr. Keno blinked first. He gave her a pinched, tight smile and held up a finger. "Excuse us for a moment," he told Mandy. The window went up with a zip.

Mandy crossed her arms and Jessica jiggled her leg and chewed nervously on a fingernail.

Mandy felt sorry for Jessica. If Jessica felt half as disappointed and disillusioned as Mandy, she was a pretty unhappy camper right now. "Johnny Buck is turning out to be Johnny Crud," Mandy muttered under her breath, making an effort not to cry.

"It's not him," Jessica argued. "It's that Mr. Keno. He's the one who doesn't want Johnny to stay. You know how it is in show business. Artistic types always wind up being kept away from their fans and pushed around by greedy managers."

"How do you know?" Mandy asked.

"*Days of Turmoil*," Jessica answered in a voice of authority. "I've been watching that soap opera for three years, and Tommy Starlight, the rock star of Pineburgh, has this manager who's always trying to break him and his girlfriend up and take his money." Jessica finished her recitation with a brisk nod of her head—like a debate captain who just delivered a slam-dunk closing argument.

Mandy pressed her lips together. Jessica was probably right. Johnny Buck was an artist and he probably left most of the scheduling details to his manager. Besides that, *Days of Turmoil* was a pretty good show. *Very realistic*, Mandy thought.

A few moments later the window rolled down a

few inches. Mr. Keno laughed, but only his mouth smiled. From the nose up, he didn't look too entertained. "I just checked with Johnny's legal people and you girls certainly know your law. Well, well, well," he murmured with a weak smile. "I hope you won't let this little misunderstanding come between us." He turned his head and spoke sharply from between gritted teeth. "Johnny, get out. You're spending the day with this young lady."

Johnny started to open the back door, but Jessica leaned forward and shut it firmly. "I want to go in the limo," she protested.

Mr. Keno smiled with his teeth still clenched. "Did the contest *say* anything about a limo?" he asked.

"No, but . . ."

"Then I guess I'll get to keep it," Mr. Keno said. His smile switched off again. "Johnny! Come on. I've got people waiting to make a deal."

Finally, after a long pause, the back door opened and Johnny Buck reemerged, still wearing his sunglasses. "I am not happy about this, Stan."

Mr. Keno handed Johnny a cell phone. "Hey! I can't change the law and we don't want a suit over this. We'll go to the hotel, unload the equipment, and set up the suites. Call when you're ready to be picked up. And don't forget, there's a press conference at one o'clock, and—"

"It's not at the hospital, is it?" Johnny asked quickly.

Mr. Keno shook his head. "No. It's in the lobby of Sweet Valley Museum."

Mr. Keno's cell phone rang and he answered it. "Keno speaking. Yeah. Yeah. I'm on my way." He saluted Johnny and the limo pulled away from the curb.

Johnny shook himself as if he were totally grossed out. "Well, at least I don't have to put in an appearance at a hospital," he muttered.

"Don't you like the hospital?" Mandy asked.

"Hospitals give me the creeps," Johnny answered.

"Then how come you're doing a benefit for one?" Mandy asked.

Johnny met Mandy's frank gaze and smiled. "I didn't say it wasn't a good cause. I'm just saying I don't like hospitals. They just freak me out a little bit, that's all." He looked at Jessica, slapped his hands, and rubbed them together. "So where do we start?"

Mandy felt her shoulders relax. A lot of people were scared of hospitals. She had begun to think Johnny was a real creep. Actually he was just a real guy.

Seven

Creaaaakkkk!

Jessica glanced up toward her bedroom. The Unicorns had raised the window slightly so that they could eavesdrop. The noise caught Mandy's and Johnny's attention too.

A burst of giggles came from the upstairs window and several noses could be seen pressed against the glass.

Johnny looked up at the house and frowned. "How many sisters do you have?" he asked.

Jessica put her hands on her hips and glared up at the Unicorns. "Just ignore them and they'll go away. Let's go to the garage and decide on transportation," she said.

Jessica threaded her arm through Johnny's and turned to smile at her docudate director. Now they were rolling. Jessica made a wide sweep of her hand. "This home is a typical California split-level, ranch-style house. It was built around thirty years ago. Notice the pink brick and the latticework along the patio wall. As we look at Sweet Valley's many points of interest, you will see several examples of that kind of . . . umm . . ." Jessica cast about for the right word. The kind of word a tour guide would use. She couldn't think of one. "Stuff," she finished.

Jessica smiled at the camera and grabbed the handle of the garage door. "We've got a lot of ground to cover and it's too far to walk, so we'll take the moped."

She flung open the garage door and gestured dramatically toward the moped. Johnny Buck circled it and kicked the wheel. "Kind of Mickey Mouse," he said. "Don't you have a car?"

"No," Jessica responded. "I'm only thirteen."

Johnny rolled his eyes. "Then I guess I'm riding a moped." He straddled the bike and turned the key in the ignition. The engine started with a roar, and he placed his boot on the pedal and tentatively pressed it. "I'm not really sure how these things . . . *yeeeoouuuwwwww!*" He screamed as the moped shot forward and into the side of the garage wall, where there were two ladders, three bicycles, and several empty paint cans stacked.

The moped fell over and Johnny tumbled off, disappearing into the heap of garage junk. Jessica ran forward and began sifting through the cans and ladders. Mandy filmed diligently, like a combat photographer. "Mandy!" Jessica begged. "Put that down and help me."

Mandy reluctantly placed the camera on the cement floor and helped Jessica. "Johnny?" Mandy called out. "Are you okay?"

Suddenly a figure shot up out of the pile and angrily tossed a can at the opposite garage wall. "Thanks a bunch!" he growled.

The back door to the Wakefield house slammed and Steven came running out. "What was that noise?" he demanded. He skidded to a stop when he saw Johnny Buck. His jaw fell open and he pointed mutely. "Are you . . ."

"Am I in one piece?" Johnny asked angrily. "Yeah, no thanks to this piece of junk." He kicked the moped.

Steven flinched as if Johnny had kicked a living thing. "What did you do to my moped?"

"Hey! You ought to be asking what it did to me," Johnny retorted.

Jessica put a restraining hand on Johnny's arm. "Johnny, I'm really, really sorry."

"Isn't anybody really, really sorry about my moped?" Steven asked.

Jessica rolled her eyes. "Steven!" she scolded. "Cut it out. It's no big deal!"

"To you, maybe. But not to me. It's my most prized possession."

Johnny lifted his hands. "Chill out, Junior. What'd this cost? Two months' allowance?" He rolled his eyes as though he couldn't believe anybody would make such a big deal out of something so small. He reached in his pocket, pulled out a big roll of cash, and peeled off several hundred-dollar bills. "Here. Allow me to replace it."

Steven's face turned red at the insult. He stared at Johnny, then at Jessica. "I can't believe you were so hot to meet the great Johnny Buck. I've met him and frankly I'm not too impressed."

Jessica turned red in anger. "I knew you would try to spoil things," she said accusingly.

"I am not trying to spoil things!" Steven protested.

"You are too," Jessica argued. "But it's not going to work. Johnny's going to pay for your stupid moped. So why don't you just go back in the house now and stop trying to ruin everything."

Steven's hurt and angry face turned white. He looked at the money in Johnny's outstretched hand and then pointedly turned his back, walking stiffly out of the garage and back to the house.

Johnny shrugged. "I don't get it. Does he want the money or not?"

"Not," Mandy said quietly from behind the camera.

Suddenly there was a high-pitched whistle. Johnny reached into his pocket and whipped out the cell phone. He opened the sleek little black instrument and answered it. "Johnny," he said curtly.

Jessica listened intently, hoping she would hear some inside show business secrets. But at that moment, she saw the Unicorns creeping out the back door and inching toward the garage.

Jessica ran outside and closed the door, shutting Johnny and Mandy inside and closing off the Unicorns' view.

"Jessica!" Kimberly protested. "We want to meet him."

"Forget it," Jessica told them. "You guys are cheating. This is my dream date, not *our* dream date. Now get lost. You're in the way. We're having a fabulous time and it's love at first sight."

"If you guys are so in love, why was he on the phone?" Lila asked.

"For your information, Lila Fowler, Johnny is on the phone with his agent telling him he's met this tremendously talented and promising newcomer to the music scene."

"Who?" Ellen asked.

Jessica pointed to her chest with her thumb. "Me."

"I said I wanted chips and salsa in my dressing room, not vegetables," Johnny said angrily. "What kind of crummy roadie are you? You don't even get the simplest stuff right. . . . What? . . . I don't *care* that veggies are better for me. I swear, if you weren't my cousin, I'd fire you. Just fix it!"

Johnny smacked the cell phone closed and noticed Mandy filming the long conversation. During the course of the call, Johnny had complained about the video games in the limo, the choice of clothes for his show, and the kind of snacks in his room.

"Cut that out," he told Mandy irritably.

"Sorry," Mandy said quietly, lowering the camera. Johnny Buck might be a real person, but he didn't seem to be a real nice person.

"Hey!" He went over and banged on the garage door. "What's going on?"

Right on cue, Jessica flung open the door and the sunlight streamed into the garage. "Okay. Everything's all arranged. I managed to convince all my *sisters* that two is company and seven is a crowd. They're gone and the coast is clear for us to take the bus."

Johnny's eyes bulged. "The bus!" He looked so horrified that Mandy couldn't help laughing.

The cell phone rang again. Johnny answered it. "Johnny. Yeah? Where's the new Jeep I ordered last week? I left instructions that it was supposed to be delivered to the house in Palm Springs. . . . Listen, I'm sick of excuses. Can you deliver it or not?"

While Johnny yelled at somebody about the custom trim he'd spent over twenty minutes picking out, Jessica sidled over to Mandy.

"Listen," she whispered. "Did you get Johnny's fall on tape?"

Mandy snorted a laugh. "Yeah. I did. That ought to be good for a few laughs later on."

Jessica bit her lip. "I know it really happened,

and we're going for a true-to-life thing, but would it be cheating posterity too much to edit it out? I mean, I really don't want Johnny to look bad. It's not that I care personally, or anything like that, but . . . well . . . we don't know who might watch this. Johnny's really helping out the hospital. We wouldn't want him to think the people of Sweet Valley were ungrateful."

Mandy sighed. Jessica had a point. "Okay," she agreed. "But I don't know how to do it on the spot. I'll edit it out a little later."

Jessica smiled in relief. "Thanks."

Johnny was off the cell phone now.

"Shall we?" Jessica asked, threading her arm through Johnny's. Johnny groaned and let Jessica lead him down the driveway toward the sidewalk. Mandy followed them, filming from a discreet distance.

The cell phone rang again. Johnny stopped in his tracks and answered it. Jessica exchanged a helpless look with Mandy.

Mandy sighed. At this rate it was going to take them all day to get to the corner. *Time to move into the proactive director role*, she told herself.

Mandy inched in closer, moving around Johnny, circling him with the camera until she was able to jostle his hand with her elbow.

"Oops," she cried when the phone fell from his hand to the pavement.

The small telephone broke into pieces and the batteries rolled down the driveway.

"Look what you did to my phone!" Johnny yelled.

"Gosh, I'm sorry," Mandy said. "But we don't have time to talk about it now. There goes the bus."

Jessica grabbed Johnny's arm and began dragging him down the street, running as fast as she could. Mandy ran behind, doing her best to film.

They arrived breathless at the bus stop on the corner. Jessica produced a fistful of change from her minibackpack and dropped it in the slot as the threesome boarded the bus.

Jessica and Johnny Buck took seats near the middle. The only other empty seat was a few rows back. Mandy sat down there and placed the camera in her lap.

The bus pulled out into the dappled street and Mandy began to feel a little more optimistic. The day had gotten off to a bad start, but maybe it wasn't fair to blame Johnny Buck. He was probably under more pressure than any of them could even imagine. Yelling about chips and salsa might seem childish, but maybe it was his way of blowing off steam.

Mandy loved to learn about people and had read the biographies of some of the great artists and composers of the last two centuries. Lots of them were temperamental and rude. She made up her mind not to judge him by the same standards that she would use to judge other people. This was her chance to film one of the greatest performers of the age. She closed her eyes and pictured herself accepting an Academy Award.

And for the best docudate . . . Mandy Miller for "Meet Johnny Buck."

A big auditorium full of movie stars jumped to their feet and applauded. Mandy hurried up a red carpeted aisle and onto a stage where she took her award and composed herself in front of a mike.

"I just want to express my gratitude to all the wonderful people who helped make this docudate possible. And I want to express my particular gratitude to Section 409 of the Games and Sweepstakes Code, which stipulates that all prizes must be awarded in accordance with the advertised terms of the contest."

"You know who that guy up there looks like?" Mandy heard someone ask in a whisper.

Mandy's daydream faded as she listened to the quiet conversation of the two girls sitting behind her.

"He looks like Johnny Buck, only shorter and not as cute," the girl continued.

Mandy couldn't resist turning in her seat. "It is Johnny Buck," she whispered.

The girls behind her lowered their eyelids and pressed their lips together, indicating that they couldn't be fooled that easily. "No way," they said together.

"Way," Mandy insisted. "It's him. I know him."

"Yeah, right," one of the girls said in a sarcastic voice. "Like Johnny Buck would really be riding the bus!"

* * *

"So when did you know you wanted to be a rock star?" Jessica asked Johnny, pitching her voice so that it would be heard by the people in front of her.

Nobody had noticed Johnny when they sat down and Jessica was disappointed. She wanted everybody in town to see her with Johnny Buck.

Johnny shrugged. "I dunno. It wasn't as if I planned it."

"You mean you didn't start out with a dream to become the great *Johnny Buck?*"

Just as she had hoped, the two people in the seat in front of them discreetly turned their heads so that they could look at Johnny.

Johnny folded his arms across his chest and slumped slightly, sitting on the base of his spine. "Things just kind of, you know, happened."

Jessica wished he would elaborate a little and add some details that would make the people sitting around them take notice. But he continued to stare out the window. Jessica racked her brains for something else to say and watched his profile. He wasn't *quite* as good-looking as she thought, but he was still very handsome.

His eyelashes fluttered and Jessica couldn't help noticing how long and thick they were. Johnny's chin fell against his chest as if he were deep in thought. Jessica held her breath. Maybe he was in the middle of the creative process. Maybe he was writing a song. Maybe he was writing a song about her!

She watched him, trying to keep absolutely still and quiet so as not to interrupt his creative flow. Then a long, gentle snore came whistling out of his nose.

The boy and girl behind Jessica giggled.

Jessica's mouth fell open in indignation. This was horrible. Johnny Buck had fallen asleep! How insulting, not to mention embarrassing.

In a panic she turned around to make sure Mandy wasn't filming. She didn't want the world to think Johnny Buck had found her so boring that he'd sat next to her and *napped*!

Luckily Mandy wasn't filming and she didn't seem to realize Johnny had nodded off. Mandy winked and lifted her hand in a wave. Jessica fluttered her fingers back and found herself staring into the amused eyes of a boy about her own age. He was sitting right behind her.

"Your friend must have had a late night," he said as another strange squealing noise came whistling out of Johnny's nose.

"He did have a late night!" Jessica said haughtily. "He's a rock star, so he's up late almost every night." She lowered her voice and acted as if she were about to confide something top secret. "He's Johnny Buck," she whispered.

The boy nodded. "Sure he is."

The girl sitting next to the boy slapped her hand over her mouth to muffle a loud guffaw.

"He *is* Johnny Buck," Jessica insisted.

But before Jessica could say anything else, the bus came to a squeaking stop and Johnny jerked awake with a particularly loud snore.

The girls in front of Jessica and Johnny burst into giggles and covered their faces. They got off and hurried toward the exit, pushing each other so that they could get off before they burst into hysterical laughter.

The boy and girl got up. Wheezing with laughter, they lurched toward the door. Jessica watched them get off the bus and felt almost sick with embarrassment.

"Come on," she said to Johnny. "This is our stop."

Johnny hauled himself to his feet with a yawn and stepped into the aisle behind Jessica and Mandy.

Jessica and Mandy stepped from the bus first, then turned to wait for Johnny. Mandy lifted her camera just as . . . the heel of Johnny's boot caught on the edge of the bottom step.

Crash!

Johnny fell forward and landed in a heap on the red clay road. A cloud of dust rose around him and he began to sneeze.

Jessica heard another round of giggles. She saw several kids, including the boy and three girls who had been on the bus, standing by the Sweet Valley Stables sign. They were pointing toward Johnny and shaking with laughter.

One of the boys came running over. He leaned over and spoke to Johnny Buck.

"Excuse me. Could I get your autograph?"

Another volley of giggles from the group by the sign pierced the air.

Jessica felt furious and embarrassed. None of them believed he was Johnny Buck. They were just trying to be funny at his expense—and Jessica's.

Johnny stood up and dusted off his jeans. He looked at the boy and sneered.

"I don't sign autographs unless you're a paying customer and you can manage to catch me backstage before I split the gig. Understand?"

His sneer and swaggering attitude suddenly made him look as composed and in control as the Johnny Buck from the videos. His voice was so arrogant and rude that the boy's smile abruptly disappeared. He backed away.

"Sorry. I uh . . . guess you really are Johnny Buck."

Jessica felt her mouth split in a wide grin. Now this was more like it.

This is horrible, Mandy thought, watching the scene from behind the camcorder. The boy and his friends had thought Johnny Buck was some wanna-be pretender. If Johnny had signed his autograph and been friendly, they would have made fun of him, thinking he was a fake.

But because he treated them badly and acted like a jerk, they were convinced he was the real thing. Boy! *That* said something sad, not just about

Johnny Buck, but about them. Why did they let Johnny behave that way?

Because he was famous and talented, that's why.

But since when was fame and talent a license to abuse people? No wonder Johnny thought he had a right to yell at the roadie who put veggies in his room instead of chips and salsa. Probably nobody ever stood up to him or made him pay a price for being rude and horrible.

But he's not like the rest of us, Mandy reminded herself. *He's a creative genius.*

Mandy swallowed her disappointment. Johnny Buck might be arrogant, rude, and clumsy, but he was a star and he was going to raise a lot of money for the hospital. Mandy made up her mind to cut him all the slack she could.

To heck with the cinema verité thing. Fiction was more fun than fact anyway—especially in Johnny's case.

"Where are we and what are we doing here?" Johnny asked Jessica.

"We're at the Sweet Valley Stables," Jessica answered. "And we're going riding."

"Forget it," Johnny told her, limping over to the pay phone near the curb.

Jessica's face fell. "But . . . but . . ."

"But nothing," Johnny snapped. "I'm not riding." He put his hand on the telephone. "Frankly, between the moped booby trap and the bus ride, I think I've had all the real life I can stand. It's too humiliating. I'm calling for a pickup. Sorry to cut our day short, but to make it up to you, I'll take you home in the limo. If that doesn't satisfy that Section 409 thing, you'll just have to sue me." He dropped a quarter into the slot.

Jessica reached over and pressed the phone, disconnecting it. "Please don't go yet," she begged. "There's so much more that I want us to see and do. We haven't even started. And I feel as if we haven't really given each other a fair chance."

Johnny gently pulled her hand away from the phone. His face softened slightly. "Sorry, kid. I'm out of here."

Mandy felt her heart harden. That sweet little face he was giving Jessica wasn't going to fool her. Apparently, creative geniuses were manipulative bullies. And Mandy had been in middle school long enough to know how to handle bullies. You had to stand up to them and bully them back.

"Excuse me," she said, pulling the tape from the camcorder and holding it up. "Just how humiliating do you think it would be if everybody in the country found out that the great Johnny Buck is a huge klutz?"

"Mandy!" Jessica gasped.

"What?" Johnny yelled.

"I filmed you hitting the gas by accident and . . . bammo . . . smashing into those paint cans." She laughed. "It's great slapstick, but not nearly as funny as you falling off the bus."

Johnny marched toward her with his hand out. "Give it to me," he demanded.

Mandy backed up. "No."

He lurched forward and Mandy tossed the tape over his head.

Jessica caught it with a little shriek of surprise. Johnny turned. "Give me that tape," he yelled, starting to run toward Jessica.

"Don't let him have it," Mandy shouted to Jessica.

Jessica dodged Johnny. "Mandy! Catch!" She tossed the tape back toward Mandy just as Johnny snatched at her hands.

Mandy backed up and zigzagged, raising another cloud of red dust with her tennis shoes. Johnny awkwardly tried to block the pass with his arms outstretched like a basketball guard. His face was red and he was perspiring heavily.

It was pretty obvious that Johnny Buck wasn't in very good shape. *He's not very coordinated either,* Mandy thought as he lurched forward and landed facedown in the dust.

Jessica ran toward him and fell to her knees beside him.

"Johnny!" she cried. "Are you all right?"

After a long moment, Johnny lifted his face and groaned in defeat. "No, I'm not all right. I've been taken hostage, forced to ride a public bus, and now

I'm being blackmailed. If you were me, would *you* be okay?"

"So you'll do it?" Jessica asked happily.

"Do I have a choice?" Johnny asked Mandy.

"No," Mandy said in a steely tone.

"Then I'll do it," he agreed.

Eight

"Okay," Mandy said to Johnny and Jessica as they waited for the groom at the Sweet Valley Stables to bring out the horse. "You two just act natural. Forget I'm here."

She lifted the camera and zoomed in on Johnny's scowling face. *Not scowling*, she told herself, *brooding*. Creative geniuses didn't scowl—they brooded.

The groom smiled and waved at the camera as he came out of the barn leading a brown mare with a short-clipped mane.

Mandy decided that they'd given Johnny a pretty hard time so far. It was time to cater a little bit to his vanity.

"Wait a minute," Mandy said. She lowered the camera.

"What's the matter?" Jessica asked.

Mandy bit her lip. "Do you have another horse? A white one?" she asked the groom.

He nodded. "Yeah. Snowflake's in the barn."

"I really think for purposes of art direction we might want to go with the white horse," Mandy explained. "What do you think, Johnny?"

Johnny rolled his eyes. "I thought we were supposed to forget you were here."

Mandy giggled. "I just can't help thinking that a handsome, brooding, dark-haired artist on a white horse will have more . . . romance and drama."

Johnny brushed his hair back off his face and looked pleased.

So did Jessica.

"Bring the white horse," he told the groom.

"Yes, sir," the groom said cheerfully. "Come on, Skipper. You're being replaced."

Jessica took advantage of the short break to brush her hair.

"Can I borrow that when you get finished?" Johnny asked.

Jessica immediately handed him the brush. "Absolutely. I'd be honored to have you use my hairbrush."

Johnny ran the brush through his tangled hair and handed it back to Jessica. "Thanks," he said shortly. He wandered over to the fence and leaned against it, staring at the landscape with a resigned expression on his face.

"Look," Jessica said, hurrying over to show Mandy her brush. "Some of Johnny's hair is in it. I'll never use this brush again. I'm going to put it away in a box and keep it to show my grandchildren."

"Pretty cool," Mandy agreed. "I hope you'll have a great docudate to show them too. Here comes Snowflake. Get ready." She lifted the camera and backed away a bit.

"Here you go," the groom said. "I'll hold her while you get on."

"We'll be riding together," Jessica told the groom.

"Fine by me," the groom chirped. "Snowflake's gentle as a lamb. You probably ought to get on first," he told Johnny.

Johnny struggled to put one boot in the stirrup. His hands fumbled slightly with the horn. Finally he got what appeared to be a good grip.

After a few tentative tugs he let out a groan and *heaved* himself up on the horse . . . only to go right over the top and land with a loud cry on the other side.

"Johnny!" Jessica ran around the horse.

Mandy followed her, filming.

Snowflake turned her head and watched the scene with large, curious eyes. She let out a waffling snort that sounded like a horselaugh.

Mandy would have laughed too—if she hadn't seen the Unicorns coming up the road on their bicycles.

"Oh no!" Jessica wailed, noticing her friends a moment later.

"Leave it to me," Mandy said quickly. She ran down the road and opened her arms, blocking their progress. They braked to a stop. "Okay, you guys, just turn right around and leave the way you came."

"*Why* can't we at least just meet him?" Lila demanded.

"Because Jessica doesn't want you to," Mandy retorted. "And neither do I. You guys agreed to stay in the background and you keep breaking your promise."

"We can't help it," Ellen whined. "We're in the grip of a power beyond our ability to control."

"Well, snap out of it," Mandy barked, taking her tone from Johnny Buck.

"What happened?" Ellen asked, craning her neck for a better view. "Why is Johnny Buck on the ground like that?"

Because he's a total klutz, Mandy thought. But she couldn't say that. Mandy began to understand why people put up with a lot from a star. They had a vested interest in making sure he looked good. If Johnny looked bad, so would Mandy and Jessica. And so would the hospital and all the people who had worked hard to make the benefit a success.

"Because he just rescued Jessica from a runaway horse," Mandy lied. "It was the most totally exciting thing I've ever seen."

The girls gasped. "Oh my gosh!" Kimberly shrieked. "Is he all right?"

"He will be. But right now he needs a little

privacy to pull himself together. Now please, don't crowd him. He's an artist and he's sensitive."

"We understand totally," Rachel said. "And we'll back off for now. But when we hit the press conference, we expect an introduction."

Mandy blinked. "Press conference? What press conference?"

Lila smirked. "The press conference at the Sweet Valley Museum. My dad was invited and he's taking us, so we'll see you guys there—whether you like it or not."

Johnny lay on the ground, breathing hard.

"Are you sure nothing's broken?" Jessica asked for the fifteenth time.

"I'm sure," Johnny snapped. "Quit asking me."

"Then why don't you get up?" Jessica asked.

"Because as long as I lie here, nothing else can happen to me," he said snidely.

Jessica felt her cheeks flush with embarrassment. The day wasn't turning out the way she imagined it at all. And she couldn't figure out why.

He sat up and looked around. "Okay. Enough's enough."

The groom leaned down and took Johnny's arm. "Let me help you."

Johnny rudely yanked his arm out of the groom's grasp. "I don't need your help," he barked, standing up and dusting off his jeans. "I need a phone. Where is it?"

The groom pointed to the office. "In there."

Johnny stalked toward the small building. Jessica trotted along behind him. "Where are you going? Aren't we going to ride?"

"I am out of here," Johnny said firmly. He walked into the office. A woman sat at a desk wearing riding clothes. She smiled and began to speak, but Johnny didn't even acknowledge her or ask for permission to use her phone. He just picked it up and began dialing. When someone on the other end answered, Johnny fired a set of instructions. "This is Johnny. I'm at the Sweet Valley Stables. Come get me—*now!*"

Jessica felt just awful. In spite of all her efforts, Johnny wasn't having a good time. "I'm really sorry things are going so badly," she said, her voice breaking. "I tried to plan activities I thought you would like, but you're having a horrible time. Is there anything else you'd like to do?"

"Hey, don't worry about it," he said grumpily. "It happens. Get your friend and I'll drop you two off on the way to the press conference."

Nine

"*What?*" Johnny yelped.

"We're coming to the press conference with you," Mandy informed him as the limo pulled out of the stable driveway.

"No, you're not," he protested.

"Yes, we are," she said. "We have to."

"Why?" he asked.

"Because the Unicorns will be there and they want to meet you," Mandy exclaimed.

"What?" This time it was Jessica who yelped.

"Lila's dad fixed it so that they could go," Mandy said. "That means we've *got* to be there."

"Who are the Unicorns?" Johnny asked.

"We're Unicorns," Jessica explained. "We're members of the Unicorn Club. There are six of us. The other four were in the house when you got there."

"Look," Johnny said. "I don't care if you're Unicorns or Tasmanian She Devils—I've had enough for one day and—"

Mandy snatched the tape from the recorder. "Image is everything," she reminded him. "When people see you fall off that horse, they're not going to talk about the Buckster, they'll talk about the Klutzster."

Johnny's brows met over his nose. "You wouldn't dare."

Mandy frowned. "Oh yes we would. You've been rude and mean."

Johnny shrugged. "Lots of rock stars are rude and mean."

"Do they snore?" Jessica asked innocently.

"I do not snore!" Johnny shouted.

"You do too," Jessica insisted gently.

"Do you have that on tape?" he demanded.

Jessica smiled. "Complete with that little whistling sound that comes out of your nose," she lied.

Johnny dropped his head into his hands. "This isn't fair," he said. "Forget it. No way. Uh-uh. I will *not* negotiate with terrorists," he insisted.

"We're not terrorists," Jessica argued. "We're fans. All the Unicorns are. We've been in your fan club for two years. We've bought all your CDs and T-shirts and posters. And are you grateful? No, you're not."

"Hey! I'm a star. I don't have to be grateful."

"And we're fans," Mandy said. "We don't have to be fair."

"What do you want from me?" he finally exploded.

"Jessica," Johnny said, gazing at her as they walked hand in hand past the photographers. "Meeting you has been an experience I will never forget. I will truly treasure this day for the rest of my life."

Jessica smiled up at him. "Johnny, I feel the same way. I can't believe that destiny hasn't brought us together sooner."

They both froze and smiled to let the photographers take pictures. Jessica saw a crew from the local TV station filming from the top of a van.

"Johnny! Over here," a photographer shouted.

"Jessica, smile," a film crew member begged.

Jessica blinked as the flashbulbs blinded them. This was so cool. She felt like a movie star arriving at the Academy Awards.

Two big guys in leather jackets that said "The Buck Stops Here" ran out of the museum and began clearing a path through the paparazzi for Johnny and Jessica.

Hand in hand, Johnny and Jessica ran up the stairs of the Sweet Valley Museum with Mandy following close behind.

Inside the lobby the waiting crowd stood behind velvet ropes. Jessica smiled and waved when she saw Kimberly, Lila, Rachel, and Ellen straining against the barrier.

Kimberly and Ellen jumped up and down, urging

her to bring Johnny over to meet them. Jessica pulled Johnny in their direction.

The girls all rustled and preened. Lila raked her fingers through her straight hair. Kimberly fluffed hers. Rachel wiped a smudge of lip gloss from the corner of her mouth, and Ellen tucked her blouse more securely into her jeans.

"Johnny," Jessica said, putting her hand on Johnny's arm. "I want you to meet some very special friends."

Johnny gave the Unicorns his famous killer smile. "Any friend of Jessica's is a friend of mine." One by one, he took their hands and gave them a firm handshake.

"This is Kimberly Haver," Jessica said. "And this is Ellen Riteman. Rachel Grant. And that's Lila," she finished with a mumble.

"Lila *Fowler*," Lila said, placing a gentle emphasis on her last name. "My father's on the board of the Sweet Valley Children's Hospital."

"Then your dad is a special kind of guy," Johnny said. His deep voice oozed with sincerity. "And I can tell by looking at you that you are a very special girl."

Lila blushed and smiled, cutting her eyes at the other girls to see how they were reacting to the compliment.

"Johnny!" A man in a suit with a "VIP Committee" button on his lapel came over and tapped him on the shoulder. "It's time to say a few words."

"Come on, Jessica," he told her, putting an arm

around her shoulders. "I want you up there with me."

The crowd of reporters, photographers, and local people applauded as Johnny and Jessica stepped onto a platform and Johnny took the mike. "Hi," he said, smiling boyishly. "I just want everyone here to know how happy I am to finally get to see Sweet Valley. I've heard it was a beautiful place, but nobody told me it was full of beautiful people. One beautiful person in particular." He gave Jessica a long and meaningful look.

The crowd applauded and Jessica heard the Unicorns sigh.

"I'm not going to talk long, because I want to save my voice for the concert. But I just want to make sure that everybody here knows that Johnny Buck's gonna rock tonight. So come out and support the cause." He lifted his fist in his trademark gesture.

The cheers and applause shook the floor beneath Jessica's feet. Johnny took Jessica's hand and they ran through the crowd, exiting the museum. Jessica looked behind her to make sure Mandy was still hanging in there. She was—dodging and darting around the other photographers and camera people like a football player. Outside the two roadies stood beside the limo. They sprang into action and opened the doors as Johnny and Jessica approached.

Johnny pulled Jessica into the limo behind him. Mandy dove in too. The doors shut with a slam and the vehicle began moving forward. Jessica could see faces pressed against the window, trying to see through the mirrored glass.

She giggled when she saw Lila's nose squashed against the window right next to Johnny. A security person pulled her and several other people away from the limo and it began to pick up speed.

Johnny let out his breath. "Well?" he said to Jessica in a sullen voice. "Are we done now?"

Jessica shook her head. "Not quite yet."

Johnny groaned and his head fell back against the seat. He pinched the bridge of his nose. "Now what?"

"Now we go swimming," Jessica said.

"Swimming? Are you nuts?"

"No. I want us to go swimming—like in your video. I'm wearing my bathing suit under my clothes."

"I'm not," Johnny pointed out.

"You can swim in your jeans."

"Do you have any idea how much these jeans cost?" he argued. "Besides, the label says dry-clean only."

"You dry-clean your blue jeans?" Mandy repeated. "That doesn't seem very . . . I don't know . . . *rugged*."

"Tell you what," he said, changing to a friendly and cooperative tone. "Let's go by the hotel and I'll get my bathing suit."

"I think he's trying to pull something," Mandy whispered.

"No, I'm not," Johnny said in a hurt tone. "I just want to get my bathing suit."

Jessica motioned to Mandy. "Let's have a conference." She turned to Johnny. "Excuse us for a moment."

Jessica shimmied into the far corner of the limo

and Mandy followed. "What do you think?" Jessica whispered, studying Johnny's profile.

"I think he's a creep," Mandy answered. "A complete phony."

"No way," Jessica cried. "He's just a little cranky because he's used to being in control. Let's give him the benefit of the doubt. He's probably tired from all that touring and stuff. We'd be pretty cranky too if we were in his shoes."

Mandy sighed. "Okay. You wanna let him off the hook?"

Jessica snorted. "No way. I'm just saying we shouldn't judge him. He's a rock star. He's used to things going right, and everything's gone wrong. But that's not his fault. It's our fault."

Mandy looked skeptical. "Whatever you say."

"Let him get his bathing suit," Jessica said. "We know he's a fabulous swimmer. A nice relaxing swim will probably put him in a good mood. Once he calms down and gets to know us, he'll be different. And then we can get him to sing with us."

"We'll go to the hotel for your bathing suit," Mandy said, talking louder so he could hear her. "But no tricks."

"No tricks," Johnny promised. He instructed the limo driver to take them to his hotel. It was only a short distance away.

"Just pull up to the front," Johnny told the driver. He turned to the girls. "Wait here. I'll run up and be right back."

"Oh no you don't," Mandy argued. "If we let you go, you won't come back."

Johnny's face turned bright red—indicating that that was *exactly* what he had been planning to do. "All right then," he grumbled. "Come on."

The girls hopped out of the limo and followed Johnny into the quiet and elegant hotel. He strode angrily toward the elevator and pushed the button for the top floor.

"How do you know where your room is?" Jessica asked.

"I stay in the penthouse wherever I go," he said. "It makes it easy to remember."

They rode up in silence. When they got off the elevator, Johnny walked across the hall, opened the door, and began to yell. "Stan!" he bellowed. "Stan, where are you? Get out here right now."

Connie, the woman they had seen that morning, came running in from an adjoining room. "Johnny! What's the matter?"

"Where's Stan?" he snapped. "I want him here right now."

"He's in the middle of a sound check at the auditorium," Connie answered. "He can't be reached. Is there anything I can help you with?"

Johnny hung his head, looking rather broken.

"Yes," Mandy answered sweetly. "Could you find Johnny's bathing suit?"

Ten

"Ahhh *choo!*" Johnny's sneeze was so loud, it attracted the attention of the people all the way on the other side of the lake.

"Stop sneezing," Mandy begged. "It makes you look so uncool."

"Mandy," Jessica scolded. "That's really mean." Jessica wished Mandy would lighten up a little.

Johnny rolled his eyes. "Thank you for your sympathy and concern. I happen to be allergic to ragweed and this dump is full of it."

"This is not a dump," Mandy argued hotly. "This is one of the most beautiful lakes in California."

"Whatever. What do you want me to do?"

"I want you and Jessica to swim together to the other side of the lake and back while I film."

Johnny rolled his eyes. "Look. I hate to tell you

this, but I'm not a real good swimmer."

Jessica felt her jaw drop. "What are you talking about? I saw you swim. I even saw you dive off a waterfall in your video."

Before Johnny could answer, his face squinched up in the most hideous expression Jessica had ever seen. "Ahhh . . . ahhh . . ."

"Let's stand back," Mandy advised under her breath. "I think this is going to be a big one."

"Ahhh . . . ahhh . . ."

Jessica backed up slightly, and when she did, a figure standing on the top of a high bluff caught her eye. He caught Mandy's eye too.

"Wow," she said. "Look at that guy. Doesn't he look familiar?"

Jessica squinted. She couldn't believe it. It was the cool guy from Sweet Valley Musicians Hall.

"It's the 'Messenger of Love'," Mandy cried, recognizing him.

As Jessica and Mandy watched, he lifted his arms and dove gracefully into the water below.

Several people applauded.

"Ahhh *chooo!*" Johnny finally exploded. The force of his sneeze was so strong, he tumbled backward and . . .

Splash!

. . . landed in the water.

Johnny's arms flailed and he let out a strangled cry of alarm.

"Think he was telling the truth?" Mandy asked.

"I mean, that he wasn't a good swimmer?"

"I don't know," Jessica said, watching him thrash around. "But it shouldn't matter. The water's only four feet deep there."

"Help!" Johnny yelled, slapping at the water with his hands.

"I think you'd better go in there and help him," Mandy said.

Jessica kicked off her shoes and ran into the lake, pushing away the tall weeds and lily pads that collected along the edge of the water.

Johnny flopped and gasped like a fish. "Help!" he gargled.

Jessica managed to grab him around the chest. It was like wrestling a dolphin. "Put your feet down!" she told him.

"Help!" Johnny screamed again.

"I *am* helping," Jessica said in a reasonable tone. "Just put your feet down."

"I'll sink," he protested.

"No you won't," Jessica argued. "*I'm* standing up and you're lots taller than I am."

"Is that Johnny Buck?" Mandy heard someone behind her ask. "I know he's in town for the hospital benefit."

She turned and saw two teenaged girls watching Jessica and Johnny with stunned and slightly disgusted expressions on their faces.

"No way," the girl's friend said. "That guy's a

total dork. *That's* Johnny Buck over there." She pointed toward the lake.

Mandy turned back toward the water and saw the "Messenger of Love" stroking gracefully toward Jessica and Johnny. Mandy ran down to the shoreline.

When the messenger got to the shallow part of the lake, he stood up and ran through the water with confident strides. He grinned at Jessica. "We meet again."

"You know each other?" Johnny gasped, allowing the messenger and Jessica to help him up to the shore.

"Of course they do," Mandy said. "He brought the good news."

Johnny turned and stared at the messenger. "What good news?" he asked slowly.

The messenger grinned. "That Jessica was the lucky winner of the 'Meet Johnny Buck' contest," he said.

Johnny's eyes narrowed angrily; then his nose began to twitch as another big sneeze came on. "You're . . . you're . . . you're . . ." When the sneeze exploded, Mandy thought she heard the word *fired* in there, but she wasn't absolutely sure.

The messenger didn't seem to be listening, though. He was looking at the gathering crowd. "Why don't we talk about this in the limo?" he suggested. "I'll go get my gear and meet you guys in the car."

The messenger jogged to the bank to retrieve his

clothes and towel. Mandy noticed that his shoulders and legs rippled with well-defined muscles. From the back, as well as from the front, he looked exactly like the Johnny Buck she was used to seeing in the videos. They could almost be related. Suddenly she had it figured out.

"Are you Johnny's brother?" she asked the messenger as he came back over to join them.

He laughed. "Nope. His first cousin. I'm Chad Bucklateski, also known as the 'Messenger of Love'."

Johnny glared at Chad from behind dripping strands of hair. "So I guess it's *you* I have to thank for getting me into this mess. Did you tell the bad seed and her little friend here they had a legal right to *torture me?*"

"Chill out," Mandy snapped. "*Sweet Talk* thought up the contest, not Chad."

"Please don't blame him," Jessica said. "It's my fault he got involved, not his."

"How do you figure?" Mandy asked.

"I hired Chad to pretend he was part of the contest," Jessica admitted. "I wanted winning to seem important. I wanted it to be special and something nobody would ever forget. The Unicorns and everybody at school were expecting a big splashy event, so I made sure they got one. I'm sorry, Mandy. I should have told you."

Mandy sighed. "It's okay. I've been gilding reality myself."

"It was the next best thing to having Johnny come himself," Jessica explained. "They do look almost exactly alike."

"That's the only reason he has a job," Johnny snarled as he climbed shivering into the limo. Chad didn't seem too insulted. He just laughed.

"Did you take care of the salsa?" Johnny demanded. "Almost drowning makes me hungry."

"I did," Chad said, toweling his curly hair. "But I still recommend veggies. You'd be a lot healthier if you ate better."

Mandy remembered the conversation Johnny had had on the cell phone in Jessica's garage. *"If you weren't my cousin, I'd fire you."*

Somebody as obnoxious and power hungry as Johnny would have no hesitation in firing anyone who crossed him—whether he was a cousin or not. That had to mean Johnny needed him for something besides roadie work!

"You're the one who stars in the videos, aren't you?" Mandy said slowly.

"He is not," Johnny yelled.

Chad winked but didn't say anything.

"Yes he is," Mandy insisted. "Now I get it. You can't ride and you can't swim. You couldn't ride a moped, much less a motorcycle." She blinked, a new and even more startling idea hitting her. "Do you even do your own singing?"

"Of course he does," Jessica insisted hotly, moving closer to Johnny and glaring at Mandy.

"That's it!" Johnny yelled. "That's the limit. When we get back to the hotel . . ."

"We'll sing with you," Mandy finished in a steely tone.

"What?" Johnny screamed.

"We'll sing with you. And Chad can film."

"No," Johnny said flatly. "No way. Not today. Not tomorrow. Not ever!"

"I don't think Johnny's mike is working," Jessica said. "I can't hear his voice." Johnny was standing right next to her. She was amazed and totally disappointed at how weak and unimpressive his voice was.

Was it possible that Mandy had been right? She hoped not. If it turned out that Johnny couldn't sing, she'd never be able to hold up her head at Sweet Valley Middle School again.

Chad put down the camera and hurried over to the pile of elaborate equipment that had been set up in Johnny's suite. He flipped a few switches. "I'm going to turn his reverb up. Voilà! Now sing a few notes, Johnny."

"I'm talkin', but you're not hearin'," Johnny belted.

With the added reverb, his voice sounded powerful and professional. He sounded like Johnny Buck the rock star. Jessica let out a long sigh of relief.

"Go ahead," Chad said to Mandy and Jessica. "I gave you guys some juice too."

Jessica and Mandy looked at each other and giggled. Jessica suddenly felt embarrassed.

"Go ahead," Chad urged. "If you make a mistake, we'll just edit it out and start over. No problem."

Jessica smiled happily. Chad was really nice. She wished Johnny would be more polite to him.

"One . . . two . . . three . . . ," Chad prompted.

The digitalized sound track began to play and Jessica took a deep breath. "I'm talkin', but you're not hearin'," she sang with Mandy.

They sounded *fantastic!* With the echo and the reverb, they sounded as if they had huge grown-up voices. Mandy's high soprano sounded clear as a bell. And Jessica's lower alto harmonized beautifully.

All those hours the Unicorns had spent listening to the song paid off, because she and Mandy knew the background parts perfectly. Their voices blended with Johnny's as if they had been singing together for years.

As they moved into the last verse, Jessica began to bob her head, throwing her hair around just like the singers on the video. Mandy did the same.

Finally they reached the last note. It was a high one. Jessica wasn't sure she could hit it. She took a huge breath. Chad took one hand off the camera and cued her.

Closing her eyes, she plunged toward the note . . . and hit it right on. She opened her eyes and grinned as she held it.

Chad turned his thumb up, congratulating her, then put his hand back on the camera.

Jessica threw back her head and held the note until the last driving beat of the song faded out.

When it was over there was a short pause; then somebody began to applaud.

Jessica looked over and saw Stan Keno standing in the doorway. He was clapping and smiling. "Very impressive," he said. His face looked really friendly and really tired. "Where did you girls learn to sing like that?"

Before either Jessica or Mandy could say a word, Johnny threw down his mike. It screeched in protest. "Where have you been?" he exploded.

"At the auditorium. There were problems with the sound system, but we got them worked out. The concert can start on time."

"I'm not so sure about that," Johnny retorted. "Do you have any idea what these kids have put me through?"

Stan held up his hands, trying to calm Johnny down. "Come on, Buckster. It goes with the territory."

"If you *ever* get me involved in something like this again, you are fired. Is that clear?" Johnny said with a snarl. "I told you doing a free concert was a bad idea. I just didn't know how bad."

"It's a good cause and one of the leading children's research facilities in the country," Stan said, rubbing his tired eyes.

"You mean, you don't *want* to do the concert?" Jessica gasped.

Johnny looked at her as though she were the biggest idiot in the world. "Would *you* want to do a free concert in a hick town like this?"

"But . . . but . . ." Jessica was so shocked and disillusioned, she hardly knew what to say.

"Johnny, it's good publicity," Stan argued.

"Good publicity? To let two little kids with a camera film me falling off a moped, falling off a horse, falling off a bus, and falling into the water?" With that, he kicked over a chair and stormed toward the other room.

"Handle this, Stan," he screamed, slamming the door shut.

Stan turned toward Jessica and Mandy. "You have a tape of Johnny doing all that?"

Mandy nodded.

Stan rubbed the back of his neck as if he had suddenly been confronted with a whole new problem. After he thought about it for a few seconds, he reached into his pocket and pulled out some money. He handed it to Chad.

"Why don't you take these two ladies down to the coffee shop and get a hamburger? I'll come down and join you in a few minutes. I'm starving and I'll bet they are too."

Chad nodded. "Sure thing, Stan. Come on, girls."

Jessica followed Chad out of the suite with a

lump in her throat. By the time they got to the elevator, tears were running down her cheeks.

Chad put his arm around her shoulders. "Come on, Jessica. Johnny says a lot of harsh things, but he doesn't mean them. Well, yes, he does. But that's just his personality."

"I'm not crying because he was mean," Jessica said. "I'm crying because he's not really Johnny Buck. He can't ride. He can't dive. And besides that, he's a total creep. All my friends think I'm having this fabulous day with the great Johnny Buck. When they find out the truth, Mandy and I both will be total laughingstocks."

The elevator door opened and they exited into the lobby. The coffee shop was located to the right. Chad herded them into the restaurant and got them settled into a booth in the corner.

A waitress came over with a pad.

"Hamburgers okay with everybody?" Chad asked Mandy and Jessica.

"Yes," Mandy answered for both of them. "With french fries, please."

"Four hamburgers with french fries and soda, please," Chad told her.

"Coming right up," she said, hurrying away in her squeaky waitress shoes.

Chad picked up his napkin and handed it to Jessica. "Listen, Jessica. Johnny Buck is a real person. He's got a lot of songwriting talent and he's a decent singer. When the equipment's in good working order, he actually sounds a lot better, but all rock stars use that stuff. As far as the rest goes—hey, movie stars don't really jump out of burning buildings or wrestle crocodiles. Why does Johnny have to be able to ride and dive?"

Jessica sniffled. "You ride and dive," she pointed out.

"Yeah, but I'm not Johnny Buck," he said with a wry smile.

"I wish you were," Mandy said.

"Me too," Chad said with a laugh. "But I can't write songs. And I can't sing them either. So we all do what we can. Including Stan."

"Is he the one who got Johnny to agree to do the benefit?" Mandy asked.

Chad nodded. "Stan's son had cancer two years ago. He was treated at the Sweet Valley Children's Hospital. Stan spent eight months putting this concert together. He's paying all the expenses out of his own pocket so that all the ticket proceeds can go to the hospital."

"I thought he was a bad guy," Jessica said quietly.

"I am a bad guy," Stan said, sliding into the booth beside them. "Did you order me a hamburger?" he asked Chad.

Chad nodded.

"Good." Stan reached back and tightened his ponytail. "Okay, ladies. Let's talk business. You've got a tape that could ruin my client's career. How do I convince you not to show it?"

Jessica's disappointment began to recede. An opportunity was presenting itself. And Jessica was very good at making the most of opportunities. "Backstage passes for all my friends, my brother, Steven, and my sister, Elizabeth," she said without hesitation.

"That's it?" Stan exclaimed.

"Weeeellll," Jessica hedged. "Not exactly."

Eleven

"Is that Johnny Buck?" A teenaged guy climbed on the fence rail and perched next to Mandy.

"Ummm," she grunted, filming Jessica and Chad as they loped around the ring at the Sweet Valley Stables. She didn't want to lie, but she didn't want to tell the truth either. *Ummm* was a pretty ambiguous answer. The guy could believe it if he wanted to—just like everybody else who watched Johnny Buck videos.

Chad's legs gripped the sides of the horse and Jessica held on tight with her arms wrapped around his waist. As they came around the ring past the camera, Chad turned his face *away* from Mandy and Jessica laid her head against Chad's back, facing the camera.

Mandy chuckled. When they spliced music into

the tape, that would look really romantic—as if Jessica was really riding with Johnny Buck.

"How are we doing on time?" Chad shouted as they cantered easily around the ring.

Mandy checked her watch. "We're right on schedule. Next stop, Sweet Valley Lake."

"My gosh! That's Johnny Buck!"

Mandy recognized the two girls who stood nearby, staring up at the bluff. They went to Sweet Valley High. They had been eighth-graders at the middle school last year.

"Who's that with him?" one girl asked.

"It looks like Jessica Wakefield," the other girl answered. "You know, she won the 'Meet Johnny Buck' contest."

"Wow! I would just die to be her right now."

Together, Chad and Jessica lifted their arms and dove from the high perch into the water. They made a graceful and athletic-looking pair. When they surfaced they shook their heads like actors in a shampoo commercial.

Mandy smiled behind the camera. This was going to make a great shot. "Okay!" she shouted. "Let's hit the editing room."

"Backstage passes?" Steven said. "That sounds pretty cool—even though at this point I'm not too crazy about Johnny Buck."

"He's not so bad," Jessica lied. She spoke softly

into the phone so that the people in the hallway of Sweet Valley Film and Edit couldn't hear her.

"After we left the house, things started going a lot better. And he said he was really sorry about the way he acted. So will you make sure you bring Elizabeth and the rest of the Unicorns to the stage door before the concert?"

"Okay," Steven agreed. "I still think he's a creep, but being backstage at any concert is totally cool. I'll round up the troops."

Jessica hung up the phone and hurried back into the editing room to join Chad and Mandy. They were laughing as they plugged the sound track into their hastily assembled video.

"It looks totally real," Mandy giggled.

Jessica watched the tape and shivered with excitement. It looked as if she and Johnny Buck were riding together and diving together.

Chad had gotten the film editor to use a lot of special effects, so when he and Jessica came out of the water and shook their heads, the water flew off their hair in slow motion and formed a sparkling halo around their heads. Each drop refracted the sunlight like a prism and created a rainbow of color.

Shots of the real Johnny and Jessica singing together were interspliced with the footage of Chad and Jessica riding and swimming. The result looked as good as any video she had ever seen on *Sweet Talk*. In fact, it looked better—because it starred Jessica Wakefield.

"The Unicorns will die when they see this," Jessica said, her heart racing with excitement.

"There's a big screen behind the band at the concert," Chad told her. "They'll show this as the opening of the act. When it's over, you can come running out from backstage and introduce him. Let's just do one more thing," Chad said to the film editor. He leaned over and whispered something and the editor nodded.

The editor tapped some keys on his computer. Then he rewound the tape. They watched the last few frames again. This time, the words *Directed by Mandy Miller* scrolled across the screen in big block letters.

Mandy lifted her hand and Jessica smacked it. "All right!" they said together.

Chad looked at his watch. "We've got to get to the auditorium." He grabbed his denim jacket and shrugged it on.

The film editor handed him the cassette and shook Mandy's hand.

"You did a good job," he said. "Very professional. Hope I get to work with you again soon." He took another cassette box off the console. "Here. Don't forget your original tape."

"Thanks," Mandy said with a smile. She tried to stuff it into her bag, but it was too crowded.

"Here, I'll take it," Jessica said, tossing it into her own backpack. "I promised to give it to Mr. Keno once Chad finished up his side of the bargain."

"Will we have time to go home and change?" Jessica asked. "We both look pretty cruddy."

Chad shook his head. "No. But don't worry. Makeup and wardrobe will fix you up."

They ran outside and jumped into the car Chad had borrowed from someone in Johnny's entourage. The auditorium was only a few minutes away. But it was close to show time and the streets were clogged with cars and pedestrians.

Finally, after what seemed like an eternity, Chad managed to maneuver the car onto the shoulder of the road. He sped along, bypassing the line of slowly moving cars. A siren screamed behind them. Jessica turned around and saw a policeman on a motorcycle signaling them to pull over.

Chad stopped the car and put down the window. The policeman climbed off his bike and walked up to the car. "Any reason why you can't wait your turn like everybody else?"

Chad held up his brightly colored "The Buck Stops Here" pass. "Sorry, officer. But I'm with the band and I need to get to the auditorium."

The young police officer's face suddenly lit up. He looked like a giddy child.

"Cool!" he said happily. "I've always wanted to do this. Follow me." He ran back toward his motorcycle and kicked it into gear. He raced past Chad with the siren on and waved his arm, signaling for Chad to follow.

Chad started the car and raced behind the

policeman along the shoulder until they reached the "reserved" entrance to the parking lot. The policeman pointed them toward it, then peeled away.

Chad waved his thanks and pulled in. "Go to the stage door. Connie's waiting for you. I'm going around to the tech booth to give them the tape. See you after the show."

He stopped the car and Jessica and Mandy got out and ran to the stage door. Steven, Elizabeth, and the rest of the Unicorns waited there. As soon as they saw Jessica and Mandy, they began to applaud.

"How was it?" Ellen demanded. "Was it the most fabulous day of your whole life? It had to be. He looked just totally in love with you at the press conference."

"I don't have time to tell you everything now," Jessica said. She knocked on the stage door. "But you guys can see for yourself when the show starts."

The door opened and Connie came out holding several plastic passes on chains. She smiled and handed them out. "Jessica and company. Welcome. You're right on time. I've got passes for everybody."

"Yea!" Rachel draped her pass proudly around her neck.

"Let's get you guys settled," Connie said, ushering them inside.

Jessica caught her breath. It was a madhouse. People rushed in every direction. Roadies, musicians, and sound people. Everybody wore a "The Buck Stops Here" T-shirt or jacket.

"Do all these people work at every concert?" she asked Connie.

Connie nodded "Yep. Three busloads of equipment. Five busloads of crew. People have no idea what goes into a show like this."

Jessica nudged Mandy. "Mr. Keno is paying for all this out of his own pocket," she whispered.

"I was just thinking the same thing," Mandy said. "It seems really horrible that Johnny will get the credit when it's really Mr. Keno who's being generous."

Connie led them into a room equipped with a line of makeup chairs. "Have a seat, Jessica. You're going to be onstage, so we want to make sure you look like a rock star."

Connie reached into a large box in the corner and removed a stack of folded T-shirts. "Here we go. Official 'The Buck Stops Here' T-shirts for everybody."

Steven and the girls eagerly pulled on the large T-shirts over their own shirts and blouses.

"Pull your passes out so that they show," Connie instructed them. "That way, everybody knows you belong backstage and you won't have any trouble with security."

They dutifully followed her instructions. A woman with bright red spiked hair and a star stuck on her cheek came hurrying in. "Who needs makeup?" she asked.

"Jessica does," Connie answered. "I'm going to take the rest of you down into the wings where you can watch everything happen. Jessica, I'll come back to get you in a few minutes."

At that moment Chad came in. Jessica gasped when she saw his face. It was white as a sheet and he actually looked sick. Wordlessly, he handed the videotape they had made to Jessica.

"Why are you giving this to me?" she asked, her voice catching in her throat. "Aren't they going to show it?"

Chad shook his head. "The concert's canceled. Johnny just called Stan. He says he's got a sore throat and he can't go on."

The Unicorns groaned.

"Oh *no*," Kimberly wailed. "How horrible."

Ellen slumped into one of the empty chairs. "He's such a wonderful guy. It must be horrible for him to have to disappoint all those little kids."

"We'll all write to him," Rachel promised Jessica and Mandy. "We'll tell him that even though he got sick, we appreciate what he tried to do."

But Jessica wasn't listening to her friends.

Stunned, she stumbled out of the room and into the hallway. Her chest was so tight she could hardly breathe. There was a pain in her heart. A terrible, horrible pain.

Chad walked into the hall. "What's the matter?" he asked. "You look as if you're going to faint."

Trembling, and sick with shame, Jessica could hardly bring herself to look him in the eye. "It's my fault," she whispered.

"What?"

"It's my fault," she said. "All my fault. He got a sore throat from falling in the water. And if I hadn't been so selfish, it never would have happened. I dragged him there because I wanted to show off to my friends. How could I have been so horrible?"

With that, Jessica burst into heartbroken sobs. She'd never felt smaller or more selfish in her whole life. The hospital, tons of sick kids, and Mr. Keno were all going to suffer because of her.

Chad leaned over and squeezed her shoulders. "Jessica, don't cry. Please. It's not your fault. Whatever you did to Johnny, he deserves."

She shook her head. "But I didn't just hurt him. I hurt a lot of other people."

"You didn't do anything," Chad insisted. He looked around as though he were afraid of being overheard. "Listen. I can't let you blame yourself. Johnny's not sick. He's just in a snit and this is his way of throwing a tantrum."

Jessica sucked in her breath. "What?"

"He's done it before," Chad said. "It makes Stan nuts. It makes us all nuts. He gets in a bad mood, decides he's not going to go on, and leaves Stan to make excuses and try to minimize the damage."

"That's horrible!"

"That's Johnny," Chad said with a resigned sigh.

"Why does everybody let him get away with it?"

"Johnny sells millions of records and videos and T-shirts and posters every year. He makes a lot of money for a lot of people, and he provides a lot of jobs for people who aren't rock stars and can't afford to walk away from a paycheck. People like me."

Jessica hugged the tape to her chest, then tore herself out of Chad's grasp and began to run.

"Jessica!" he shouted. "Jessica, where are you going?"

She continued running toward the exit, fresh tears spilling down her cheeks. She practically threw herself at the stage door, barreling through it.

"The buck stops here," she shouted over her shoulder, almost choking on the words.

Twelve

Jessica snuck past the hotel doorman and raced toward the elevator.

A bell captain spotted her and started in her direction. "Young lady! Young lady! Stop!" Jessica managed to jump into the elevator and press the penthouse button just in time.

The elevator doors closed on the bell captain's agitated face. "You're not supposed to . . ."

Jessica never heard the end of his sentence. But she didn't care what she wasn't supposed to do. She was so angry. She had already "borrowed" Stan's limo and driver to get her from the auditorium to the hotel, and she was ready to break every rule in the book.

When the elevator opened she raced across the hall and rapped on the door of Johnny's room.

"It's about time you got here," she heard Johnny yell from inside the suite. "You guys have the crummiest room service in the whole coun—" The door swung open and Johnny broke off with an angry shout when he saw Jessica.

He tried to slam the door shut, but Jessica managed to insert her shoulder and shoe into the suite. Johnny pressed against his side of the door and tried to force her out. Jessica pressed back as hard as she could.

Luckily Johnny Buck had been eating too much junk food. Even though he was taller than Jessica, he wasn't all that strong and he was in terrible shape. Jessica had more stamina. After about ten seconds of shoving, Johnny gave up and stepped back.

The door flew open and Jessica practically fell into the suite. Johnny paced angrily, his silk robe fluttering around him. "Didn't they tell you I'm sick?"

There was a knock on the door frame. A puzzled-looking room service waiter stood there with a tray.

"Excuse me, Mr. Buck. Your dinner."

"Bring it in," Johnny ordered angrily.

The waiter came in and placed the tray on a table. He removed the silver dome that covered the large plate. Johnny's dinner consisted of a large steak, a lobster, two baked potatoes with shredded cheese and bacon bits, and a big piece of key lime pie.

"Take that away," Jessica said, covering the plate back up with a clang. "Mr. Buck is a sick man. That heavy food might kill him. He needs a little clear broth and some tea."

The waiter bowed and picked up the tray.

"Don't listen to her," Johnny yelled. "Leave that here."

The waiter bowed again and quickly exited.

"Look, little girl," Johnny said as soon as the waiter had left. "You've had your fun. Now what do you want?"

"I want you to go over and do the concert."

"I'm sick," he repeated.

"You are not," she yelled. "You're faking it. Just like you fake everything. But that's okay. I can accept that you're not really a rider. I can accept that you're not really a swimmer. I can even accept that you're not really a very good singer. But what I can't accept is that you're not really a human being!"

Johnny turned his back and stared stonily out the window.

"You're famous for being a singer and an athletic guy. You know what I'm famous for?" she pressed. "*I'm* famous for being selfish."

He turned, surprised. "What?"

She nodded. "I'm not very proud of it, but that's just sort of my thing. I love to be the center of attention. I love to be the star. And I'll even play dirty tricks on my friends to push them out of the spotlight so that I can get more of the glory."

Jessica went over and stood beside him. "You know, when I came over here, I thought you were the biggest creep in the whole world. But you're not. You're like me, really. You just get away with a lot more."

That got a reluctant laugh out of Johnny.

Encouraged, Jessica took the two tapes out of her backpack. "If *I* can put somebody else's feelings ahead of my own, then I know you can do it too." She put the two tapes on the table. "Here are both tapes. The one Mandy made and the one we made in the studio. You can have them and burn them if you want to. Just please, *please* do the concert."

Johnny stared at her. "You'd really give up the chance to be a star tonight?"

She nodded. "Yes. Because the important thing is the hospital. Coming through for the people who are the real stars. People like Mandy."

"Mandy? How does she figure in this?"

"Mandy is a cancer survivor," Jessica told him softly. "Just like Mr. Keno's son."

Johnny's mouth fell open and the color drained from his face. "Stan's son had *cancer?*"

"Two years ago. Didn't you know?"

Johnny sank down in a chair and put his hands on the top of his head. He let out a long, shuddering breath. "No," he said finally. "I didn't. Back when I was just starting out I used to spend a lot of time over at Stan's house with his family. But for the past couple of years things have been getting more and more crazy. . . . I can't believe I didn't know."

"Did you know he was paying all the concert expenses himself?" Jessica asked.

Johnny winced as if he were in pain. "No. I had no idea. Stan's a savvy deal maker and I just assumed this gig was a publicity stunt and the record company was paying for it."

"It seems weird that you wouldn't know something like that," Jessica marveled.

"Stan Keno made me what I am. But when things really started to pick up for me, I started to think of him as a business associate. I guess I forgot that he was a person too."

"Everybody's somebody," Jessica whispered. "Even if they're a nobody. Like me."

Johnny lifted his face and reached out for her hand. "You're not a nobody. You're a real important somebody. Meeting you has been an experience I will never forget."

Jessica's heart hammered against her chest. For the first time all day, Johnny looked like the romantic hero she had always believed him to be.

"I will truly treasure this day for the rest of my life," Johnny continued. "When I said it at the press conference, I didn't mean it. But I do mean it now. If it weren't for you, I might never have found out what a creep I really am."

The little clock on the desk began to ting. Johnny jumped up and ran into the bedroom. "Call downstairs and order the car," he shouted. "I'll be ready in twenty seconds."

Mandy huddled miserably in the wings behind some large amplifiers. She peered out at the sea of faces in the Sweet Valley Auditorium. The front

row was full of kids with caps, wigs, and funky
scarves covering their bald heads. They were pa-
tients from the hospital. And they were waiting for
their hero, Johnny Buck.

Tears rolled down Mandy's cheeks. They were
going to be so disappointed. Everyone was going
to be disappointed.

The Unicorns stood on the other side of the stage,
talking with some of the band members. They were
all very concerned about Johnny. Mandy wondered
how concerned they would be if they knew the truth
about him. They never would, though. A deal was a
deal. And she had given Mr. Keno her word.

"Stan!" a concert official said. "The show was
supposed to start twenty minutes ago. We've got to
make a decision."

Mandy turned and watched Mr. Keno and the
other man talk. Mr. Keno looked really old and tired.
He had big bags under his eyes. Mandy thought he
looked as though he were going to cry. "I'd hoped he
might change his mind. But you're right. It's not fair
to keep these folks here if there's not going to be a
show. I'll go out there and tell them."

Mandy felt so sorry for Mr. Keno when he
walked out on the stage. Several people applauded.
But several others began to chant . . . "Johnny Buck!
Johnny Buck! Johnny Buck!"

Mr. Keno took the mike off the stand and held
up his hand for silence. "May I have your attention
please? I need to make an announcement. Johnny

Buck sends his sincerest apologies and deeply regrets that . . ."

". . . that he's late!" Another voice cut Mr. Keno off and boomed through the auditorium.

Mandy let out a scream along with the audience when Johnny Buck ran onstage in tight blue jeans, a black leather jacket, and a pair of black boots. He lifted his fist and everybody in the audience jumped to their feet and cheered.

"The buck stops here," he yelled. "But the fight against cancer is just getting started. Helllloooo, Sweet Valley!"

The audience roared its response.

Tears of happiness and relief poured down Mandy's cheeks. Mr. Keno ran off the stage and stood beside her. He was crying too.

"He came through," Mandy choked. "He came through."

Mr. Keno reached for Mandy's hand and squeezed it.

The house lights went down, the drummer hit the snare, and suddenly the auditorium was rocking. Johnny danced and sang even better than he did in his videos.

Mandy still didn't like him, but she had to admit—she was impressed. The Unicorns stood on the other side of the stage with Steven and Elizabeth, clapping their hands to the music and dancing with some of the stagehands.

Jessica stood in front of them, almost onstage

but just hidden by the curtain. By the dazed expression on her face, Mandy could tell Jessica felt as if she had entered a dream world.

Finally, after an hour of slammin', jammin' rock 'n' roll, Johnny wiped his sweating brow and cued somebody in the wings. A large screen dropped down behind the band.

"I'd like to dedicate this next song to someone very special. My favorite Sweet Valley gal pal, Jessica Wakefield."

Mandy broke out in head-to-toe goose bumps as Johnny sang along to the videotape she and Chad had made. Jessica looked gorgeous, and it was virtually impossible to tell the difference between Johnny and Chad.

All too soon, the song came to an end, and Mandy saw her name scroll down the screen in huge letters. The Unicorns all applauded wildly. When Johnny reached out his hand and Jessica came running onstage to join him, the whole auditorium jumped up and gave them a standing ovation.

Johnny cued the drummer again and the band began to play the song that Mandy, Jessica, and Johnny had sung this afternoon. Johnny and Jessica sang the first verse together; then Johnny held out his hand and pointed right at Mandy.

Mandy pointed to her chest. "Me?" she mouthed.

Johnny and Jessica both nodded and motioned her out.

Shyly, Mandy stepped onstage. Jessica invited

her to share her mike, and pretty soon, Mandy was singing along. They sounded even better than they had in the suite. The lights were shining in her eyes, so she couldn't see the audience, but she could *feel* them out there. Never in her whole life had she felt as alive as she did this minute.

Johnny ran offstage and came back on, leading Rachel, Lila, Ellen, and Kimberly. He clapped his hands together, telling the audience it was time for everybody to participate.

The audience roared again.

Johnny ran offstage and returned with Steven and Elizabeth. Both of them looked red-faced and shy but really pleased to be onstage.

The band cranked up the tempo and the whole group onstage began to sing and sway to the music. Mandy shook her head, letting her hair fly in every direction.

Finally the band hit the last note. Some of the singers hit it and some of them didn't. But it didn't matter. It was the most beautiful music Mandy had ever heard in her whole life.

Thirteen

"This is *so* unbelievable!" Ellen looked around the crowded hotel suite with eyes as big as saucers. "The whole Unicorn Club is actually partying with Johnny Buck after his concert! Pinch me."

Jessica laughed and happily obliged, clamping her fingers down on the fleshy part of Ellen's arm.

"Ouch!" Ellen shrieked. She blinked her eyes, looked around, and broke into a grin. "Cool! It's *not* a dream. It's real. So I guess those sandwiches and sodas are real too. That's really good because I'm starving."

Jessica laughed again and watched Ellen move toward the lavish buffet that had been set up in Johnny's suite for the band, the crew, and the guests. Lila and Rachel stood near the guacamole and chips talking to Chad and flirting. Steven,

Elizabeth, and Kimberly were looking at the fancy recording equipment.

Near the window, Johnny Buck and Stan Keno talked quietly and looked out at the view. Jessica moved through the crowd until she stood at Johnny's elbow. When he saw her there, he put his arm around her shoulders.

"Jess, I was just telling Stan that I owe you big time. How would you feel about taking all your friends home in the limo?"

"That would be nice," Jessica agreed. "But I'd really rather have something else."

"Name it," Johnny said generously.

"I want you to promise me something," Jessica told him solemnly.

"Uh-oh." Johnny's face turned comically wary.

"You really don't get enough exercise," Jessica told him. "I think swimming and riding lessons would be a great way for you to get into shape and then you would be more, you know, like Johnny Buck. And you can play yourself in your videos."

Johnny and Stan both threw back their heads and laughed.

"Is that all?" Johnny asked.

"Nooo," Jessica said. "You should eat more vegetables and less junk."

Chad came over and joined the group. "What's so funny?" he asked.

"Jessica's trying to put you out of a job," Stan answered with a smile. He sketched in the details of Jessica's health and fitness plan for Johnny, and Chad began laughing too.

"Well, he can hire me as his personal trainer," Chad said brightly.

"All right!" Stan, Johnny, and Jessica all said at once.

Jessica lifted her arm to high-five Johnny, but he ignored her outstretched hand and leaned over to kiss her on the cheek.

"Thank you, gal pal," he whispered.

Jessica blushed and felt goose bumps pop out from her toes to her fingertips. Johnny Buck had actually kissed her!

She heard applause from the other side of the room. Jessica's face flushed when she realized that the Unicorns had been watching. But she couldn't help feeling pleased—especially when she saw that Mandy was standing on the sofa with the video camera.

It was a great moment in Unicorn history!

"Copies for everybody," Jessica said two days after the concert. "Compliments of Johnny Buck. He had them copied during the concert and Chad brought them to my house yesterday." She handed each girl her very own copy of the video starring Jessica and Johnny (and Chad).

"I feel like Cinderella," Ellen said mournfully. "Two nights ago I was onstage with Johnny Buck. And now I'm back at school eating mystery meat loaf. I can't believe it's all over."

"The fight against cancer is never over," Mandy reminded her, taking a bite of her sandwich.

"I know that," Ellen retorted. "I just wish Johnny Buck and all those great people could have stayed in town another day."

"Me too," Kimberly said. "Then maybe we could have all gone swimming and riding with him."

Jessica caught Mandy's eye and swallowed a laugh. The Unicorns didn't know how lucky they were to still have all their illusions intact.

"By the way," Lila said. "Where are all the out-takes? Where's the footage you didn't use?"

"I don't know how it happened, but it just got lost," Jessica said, opening her eyes wide to express her bewilderment. "Right, Mandy?"

"Um . . . right," Mandy said. She covered her mouth with a napkin. Her shoulders shook slightly and Jessica knew she was trying not to giggle.

"Next time, put me in charge," Kimberly asserted. "That's the kind of thing it takes a responsible and mature person to really handle."

"Oh, like you're really responsible and mature," Ellen said, rolling her eyes.

"I am," Kimberly insisted. "Don't forget—I'm the only eighth-grader in the club."

The Unicorns all hooted and laughed.

"How could we forget?" Rachel asked with a grin. "You remind us at least once a day."

"One of these days you guys will learn to appreciate me," Kimberly said with a haughty lift of her chin. "And it might be sooner than you think."

Kimberly's ready for some real, sophisticated fun and she's about to lead the Unicorns on their most fabulous adventure yet. But once the excitement is over, will the Unicorn Club ever be the same again? Find out in THE UNICORN CLUB #23, **Trapped in the Mall.**

SIGN UP FOR THE SWEET VALLEY HIGH® FAN CLUB!

Hey, girls! Get all the gossip on Sweet Valley High's® most popular teenagers when you join our fantastic Fan Club! As a member, you'll get all of this really cool stuff:

- Membership Card with your own personal Fan Club ID number.
- A Sweet Valley High® Secret Treasure Box
- Sweet Valley High® Stationery
- Official Fan Club Pencil (for secret note writing!)
- Three Bookmarks
- A "Members Only" Door Hanger
- Two Skeins of J. & P. Coats® Embroidery Floss with flower barrette instruction leaflet
- Two editions of *The Oracle* newsletter
- Plus exclusive Sweet Valley High® product offers, special savings, contests, and much more!

Be the first to find out what Jessica & Elizabeth Wakefield are up to by joining the Sweet Valley High® Fan Club for the one-year membership fee of only $6.25 each for U.S. residents, $8.25 for Canadian residents (U.S. currency). Includes shipping & handling.

Send a check or money order (do not send cash) made payable to "Sweet Valley High® Fan Club" along with this form to:

SWEET VALLEY HIGH® FAN CLUB, BOX 3919-B, SCHAUMBURG, IL 60168-3919

NAME_____
(Please print clearly)

ADDRESS_____

CITY_____ STATE _____ ZIP_____
(Required)

AGE _____ BIRTHDAY_____ /_____ /_____

Offer good while supplies last. Allow 6-8 weeks after check clearance for delivery. Addresses without ZIP codes cannot be honored. Offer good in USA & Canada only. Void where prohibited by law.
©1993 by Francine Pascal   LCI-1383-123